CHANGING LANES

by Kathleen Long

The characters and events portrayed in this book are fictitious. Any similarity to real persons, living or dead, is coincidental and not intended by the author.

Text copyright © 2013 Kathleen Long

Published by Amazon Publishing
PO Box 400818
Las Vegas, NV 89140

ISBN-13: 9781611099454
ISBN-10: 1611099455
Library of Congress Control Number: 2012921364

CHANGING
LANES

There are moments in life when the expected becomes the unexpected, the known crosses the threshold to the unknown, and the everyday turns to treasure.

For Bill, who celebrated the unexpected, marveled at the unknown, and discovered treasure along each step of the journey. I love you.

For every shared moment imprinted on my mind, I wish we had one thousand more.

Until we meet again.

"*We must be willing to let go of the life we have planned, so as to have the life that is waiting for us.*"

—Joseph Campbell

CHAPTER ONE

— — —

There are times in life when a woman thinks to herself, *My plans are working beautifully.*

I pulled into the gravel drive of my parents' home, looked in the rearview mirror to the suitcase and boxes of personal belongings piled on the rear seat of my car, and sighed.

This was *not* one of those times.

"Pond-sucking bugs," I muttered.

My plans for the day had included moving from my cookie-cutter condo in South Jersey to the fixer-upper Victorian my fiancé, Fred Newton, and I had purchased on Second Avenue in Paris, New Jersey.

They had not included being chased off by a swarm of termites and my exterminator's warning about structural damage.

I may not be a builder, Abby, but I know termites.

There was only one thing to do with temporarily derailed plans. Fix them.

Step one was telling Fred we wouldn't be meeting at our new house.

I glanced at the time on my cell phone. Fred had promised to be in Paris by four o'clock, and it was now four forty-five and I still hadn't heard a word. Even though the lease on his Hoboken

1

apartment wasn't up for another month, we'd planned to use this weekend to celebrate the beginning of our new life together, starting with dinner tonight. I frowned.

Fred was never late. *Never.* His punctuality happened to be one of the things I loved about him.

I pulled up his number and waited patiently as his voice mail kicked in.

"Hey, honey," I said, raising my voice over the sound of hammering coming from my parents' roof. "I'm at Mom and Dad's instead of our house. I'll explain later. Call me back."

I disconnected, tucked the phone in my pocket, and pushed open the driver's-side door to step outside. I wrangled my suitcase out of the backseat and fought with the button to release the handle.

The afternoon had grown warm, one of those spring days that stuns you with its brightness, lightness, and fragrances—flowers in bloom, freshly cut grass—as if all was right with the world, when, in fact, it wasn't.

The hammering noise came again, and I squinted up into the late-day sun to get a better look at the source.

And there stood Mick O'Malley, the boy next door who hadn't been the boy next door since partway through our senior year of high school.

"Mick?" I asked in disbelief. "What are *you* doing here?"

"Nice to see you, too," he called out over the side of the roof. "Long time no see. You're looking well. How's your mother? Any of those more traditional greetings would do just fine, Halladay."

My left eye twitched, and I pressed a finger against the offending lid while doing my best to pretend I was merely shielding my eyes from the sun.

Mick climbed down the ladder a man, a far cry from the eighteen-year-old boy he'd been when I'd last seen him. He'd been one of my closest friends back in school. *Been* being the key word in that sentence. "Seriously," I asked, "what are you doing here?"

He stepped into my line of vision, and I stared at him, hoping my look would convey the fact that I'd forgotten nothing about the way he'd left Paris. The way he'd left me.

His features had aged even better than I'd imagined, and I found that more annoying than the fact I felt compelled to tell him everything about my day.

Old habits die hard.

"Your dad asked me to fix the roof." Mick wiped a hand over his forehead and through his dark hair, leaving the strands in a state of utter disarray.

"So you came back to town for that?" I asked incredulously.

Mick looked like he wanted to laugh at me, but he didn't. "No, Halladay. I've been back."

"But…why didn't he hire someone?"

Mick's smile turned smug. "He did."

"I thought you were some hotshot architect out west?"

I regretted the question the moment the impact of my words registered on Mick's face. His grin faded. His features tightened. The light in his eyes vanished.

"No," he said simply.

He'd never been one for explanation, and I knew better than to push.

"How about you?" His gaze shifted again, a small measure of light returning to his vivid blue eyes. "I hear you've been encouraging the world to be nice?"

I *had* been, until my editor's early morning call had ended my eight-year stint as a syndicated advice columnist.

3

"You know me," I lied, ignoring the pit in my stomach where my editor's words echoed. *Falling readership. Changing tastes. Sign of the times.* "If you can't say anything nice, don't say anything at all," I said with a forced smile.

Now visions of a rapidly disappearing savings account danced in my head.

Mortgage payments. Termite treatment. Unemployment.

Mick tipped his chin toward my suitcase. "You moving in?"

"Temporarily," I answered. *Very* temporarily.

If I couldn't move into the yellow Victorian in the morning, I'd stay with Fred at his apartment an hour north. After all, I wouldn't be commuting to work anymore.

"Thought your new house was over on Second?"

As usual in Paris, everyone knew everything.

"Sadly, so are most of the termites in New Jersey," I said.

Mick chuckled, and I ignored the warmth of familiarity the sound ignited in me.

He shook his head. "Only you, Halladay."

"Good to see you've still got that whole empathy thing working for you."

"Ouch." He faked a shudder. "I always did bring out your bad side."

No kidding. "You could bring out Tinker Bell's bad side."

Mick took a step toward me, and I held my ground, ignoring the urge to run inside. "Tinker Bell wouldn't complain." His voice had dropped low, dangerously low.

My phone rang, bleating out a poorly rendered electronic version of "Going to the Chapel."

Fred. Finally.

Mick's dark brows lifted. "Saved by the bell."

"You or me?" I asked at the exact moment I pressed the screen to answer my phone.

"You or me what?" Fred asked.

I breathed a sigh of relief, never happier to hear my fiancé's safe, solid tone than at that moment.

"Hi, honey." I took great satisfaction in watching Mick frown. "You won't believe the day I've had. Are you running late?"

"That's why I'm calling, actually. I can't make dinner."

"Meet me at the Pub later, then. We need to talk about the house."

"No, I can't make it."

Our normally flawless connection crackled with static, and I turned my back to Mick and frowned. "Why not?"

"Tonight isn't going to work."

Fred spoke the words with less emotion than usual, and when you were Fred, that was saying something.

Somewhere deep inside my brain a tiny alarm bell began to chime, but after dealing with termites, termination, and Mick, I was a quart low on patience. Mick moved into my peripheral vision, so I did another pivot to avoid his eavesdropping stare.

I dropped my voice to a whisper. "What are you talking about?"

"I'm not sure, Abby."

Fred's tone remained flat, and Mick stepped directly into my line of vision, concern plastered across his face.

My brain did a somersault, and I turned my back again, feeling like a marionette on a string.

"What's wrong?" I whispered into the phone, forcing the words past the panic clawing its way up my throat.

"I'm bored," Fred answered.

"Bored? We're getting married in two months and we just settled on our new house."

"Exactly."

I took a deep breath and focused on being supportive. I was planning to spend my life with this man. Surely I could find a way to help him through a boredom crisis. "Do you have any plans for how to deal with this?"

"I'm in Paris."

"Great. Then meet me at my parents' or the Pub and we can talk about it."

"France," he said.

I took a sideways step to regain my balance.

Mick grasped my elbow and I jerked my arm away so sharply I staggered three steps in the opposite direction.

Nervous laughter started low in my belly and spiraled upward and outward until I laughed so hard a tear slid down my cheek. "You're in Paris, *France*?"

"See?" Fred answered. "You think that's funny. For your information, I drove to JFK last night and took the first plane out."

No wonder he was late.

"You're in *France*? I'm dealing with termites and losing my job and you're in France?"

My tone bordered on yelling, but I caught myself, dropping my voice and shifting even farther away from Mick's curious stare.

"Termites? And you lost your job? Abby, what—" He stopped himself, and a long-suffering sigh filtered across the line. "No, I'm sorry—I just don't have the energy for this right now. Give me some time, Abby. Please."

My mouth went dry. The soft ringing of my mental alarm turned into a full-out clanging bell. I stared down at the tasteful diamond on my left hand and considered the ramifications of what my typically predictable Fred was saying.

The line clicked dead in my ear, but I made no move to press the disconnect button. Mick's hot stare burned into the back of my head.

I'd be darned if I was going to let Mick know my fiancé had just hung up on me…from Paris. The *real* Paris.

"Okay, that sounds like a great opportunity," I said. "Sure, sweetie. I'll talk to you later tonight. I love you, too."

Anger and disbelief swirled inside me, but I pasted on my best I-am-loved-and-cherished smile and disconnected, all the while wishing for a magic reset button to return things to the way they'd been this morning—prior to the infestation discovery, the end of my column, and Fred's sudden departure for Paris, *France*.

Suddenly, I was having trouble wrapping my brain around what was left of my life.

Mick's dark brows pulled together as if he had a window into my jostled mind. "Trouble in paradise?"

I shook my head and gave a quick shrug. "Nope. Fred—my fiancé—was offered the opportunity to do some consulting in Paris, France, so he jumped at the chance."

"So he's a bit of a risk taker?" Mick asked.

I nodded. "Regular daredevil." I swallowed loudly.

Mick reached for my elbow, and his touch brought back a rush of memories. Racing bikes. Climbing trees. Going to jail.

Tears clouded my vision, and for a split second I wasn't sure whether they were for Fred…or for the past.

Emotions crashed inside me.

The man I thought I'd be seeing that night had left the country. Hell, he'd left me.

The man I thought I'd never see again stood before me like a ghost from years gone by.

My thoughts slammed to a halt as a short blur raced across the lawn and hit me at full speed—coppery hair, hot-pink leggings, and phony Southern accent flying.

"Abby, sugar. When did you get home?"

My baby sister, Melissa, born as late in the marriage of Madeline and Buddy Halladay as I'd been born early, had seen ten minutes of *Gone with the Wind* a week earlier, and had been channeling a middle-aged Southern woman ever since.

I pulled her up onto my hip, relishing the feel of her small arms around my neck and the scent of her favorite strawberry shampoo. "How about a hug?" I asked.

"Anything for you, sugar." Missy squeezed her arms tight, then allowed me to breathe as she turned her attention to Mick. She batted her ridiculously long eyelashes. "Afternoon, Mr. Mick."

Mick shot Missy a wink, then bowed. "Afternoon, Miss Melissa."

I rolled my eyes and turned toward the front door. "Good talk, Mick. Have a nice day."

"I declare," Missy whispered into my ear, "that is one fine man."

I stumbled on the bottom step as we headed for the wraparound porch. "I think we need to talk to Mommy about upping the parental controls on the television."

But as I reached the front door and sneaked a glimpse at Mick O'Malley climbing back up the ladder, I had to admit my little sister had a point. My old friend had grown into a man...an apparently fine man.

My left eye twitched again, and I refocused on the front door and my imminent reentry into my childhood home.

My chest tightened. Moving home—no matter how temporarily—had never been part of my long-term plan. But then again, nothing about this day had been part of my plan.

I stepped into the house, standing for a moment in the center hall, letting my eyes adjust to the change in light. Missy catapulted out of my arms. Frankie, the middle of we three Halladay sisters, sat on the bottom step of the impeccably painted staircase that led to the home's second floor. She'd pulled her unnaturally black hair into a severe ponytail and sat, chin on fists, visibly seething.

Her appearance drew a sharp contrast to the vase of fresh flowers my mother had set on the hall credenza. Freshly picked tulips in shades of lavender, pink, and yellow brightened the space. My mother took pride in the house and her garden, making both the showcase of the block. I'd hoped to someday make the yellow Victorian shine like my parents' home, but now...

I studied Frankie. Today's choice of clothing included her preferred shades of black, black, and black.

"Tough day?" I asked.

Frankie raised her focus long enough to shrug.

I thought about sitting down beside her to find out what was going on in her world, but as usual, she looked more interested in being left alone.

"Where's Mom?" I asked.

Frankie jerked a thumb at the kitchen door, then stared back at the space between her feet. I followed the sound of Mom's humming, my frazzled nerves instantly soothed by the off-key tune.

I hesitated in the doorway of the kitchen, taking in the sight of my mother in the split second I had before she sensed my presence.

She stood at the kitchen sink peeling apples, stunning in a fitted black shirtdress, perfectly pressed floral apron, perky blond-on-blond precision haircut, and coordinated turquoise jewelry.

My mother was impeccable, from her perfectly decorated house to her flawless sense of style.

Then she turned, her smile spreading wide across her face. "Sorry about the termites, honey, but it's good to have you home, even if it's only temporary."

She crossed the room and planted a kiss on my cheek, holding her wet hands wide so as not to moisten my blouse. When she straightened, a vertical crease dented the patch of skin between her eyes. "What's wrong?"

I shrugged, doing my best to hide my dismay. The woman missed nothing. Never had. Never will.

"Termites, Mom. Isn't that enough?"

Her eyes narrowed. Then she shook her head and pursed her lips. "You never could tell a lie, sweetie. Fess up."

I took a deep breath. "They canned my column."

My mother clucked her tongue. "Their loss. You'll find something even better."

She took a backward step and studied me from the top of my head to the tips of my toes and back again, tilting her head first to one side, then the other.

"What else?" she asked.

I shrugged as if I had no idea what she was talking about. "Why does Dad have Mick O'Malley up on the roof? And why did no one tell me he was back in Paris?"

She dried her hands on her apron, then lifted my chin with two fingers. "Don't change the subject, Abigail." She arched two perfectly plucked brows. "Is it Fred?"

Despite my best efforts, tears welled in my eyes. "He went to Paris." I spoke the words on an exhale.

"How is that a problem, sweetheart?" she asked.

"France," I whispered, shifting my focus to the ceiling, the wall, anywhere but the depths of her all-knowing brown eyes. "Paris, France."

My mother squinted.

This was big. The woman typically showed no emotion in her features other than bliss and contentment.

"He said he was bored." A tremble started inside me, and I worked to keep my voice steady and my tears in check. "He needs some excitement."

"So he went to Paris?"

I nodded.

"And what about the..."

A fraction of color drained from my mother's flawless cheeks. She didn't have to finish her sentence. I knew exactly what she was thinking. I was thinking the same things.

What about the house? The wedding in two months? What about the down payment your father and I put on the Bainbridge Estate ballroom? What will the neighbors think?

Suddenly I needed space. I needed to be alone. I needed to wrap my brain around the fact that the most stable man I'd ever known had flown off to the most romantic city in the world... without me.

I kissed my mother's cheek and turned for the hall. "I'll fix this. All of this. Don't worry."

"You always do," Mom called after me as I headed up the steps. Frankie had vanished, abandoning her sulking post at the bottom of the stairs.

I pushed open the door to my bedroom and stared. The sight never ceased to amaze me. My academic awards still lined the shelf. My lone varsity letter remained pinned to the weathered bulletin board. A faded snapshot of the Terrific Trio—Jessica, Destiny, and me—hung taped to the wall. My room looked exactly as it had when I'd left for college, and although I was glad to have a place to stay tonight, I couldn't help but wonder, yet again, why my mother hadn't redecorated.

I stared at my four-poster bed and the Rutgers University pillow placed perfectly against the headboard.

My body was in motion before my brain kicked into commonsense mode. I took a quick double-step and jumped, just as I'd jumped countless times before. I twisted in midair, sailing onto the bed where I'd once spent hours thinking about life, sorting out problems, planning for the future.

Then I landed.

The wood supports gave way. The mattress and box spring crashed to the floor. The house shook with a force that no doubt sent the neighbors scrambling to report an earthquake.

I stayed sprawled on my back, staring up at the dark-blue ceiling and stars I'd painted years earlier—bright spots of metallic and iridescent paint designed to remind me that even if I aimed for the moon and missed, I'd land among the stars.

Some vertebrae in my back made a noise I knew couldn't be good.

I'd landed among the stars, all right, with termites in my house, my column on the skids, and my fiancé in France.

I expected my mother to yell, but I should have known better.

Instead she merely called up to me, her June Cleaver, singsong tone intact, "Everything all right, dear?"

"Perfect," I answered.

I pulled my Rutgers University pillow over my face and let my tears come.

Just perfect.

CHAPTER TWO

— — —

A few hours later, I sat at my parents' dining room table and pushed my mother's meat loaf around my plate. Madeline Halladay had never met a spice she liked, relegating most seasoning purchases to sit on the kitchen counter until their contents turned pale khaki. Her meat loaf—like every dinner she cooked—tasted less than exciting.

Maybe Fred was right. I'd grown up in a house with boring food—maybe my entire life wasn't far behind.

Silverware clattered against my mother's fine china as my family dined in silence. No one said a word.

Quite frankly, they were freaking me out.

I'd heard my mother, father, and grandmother speaking in hushed tones in the kitchen earlier. I was quite certain Mom had filled them in on the state of my life. Yet, here we sat saying nothing.

Occasionally one of them would glance in my direction, looking away quickly if our eyes met.

You'd think someone would ask me how I felt. Maybe they were too afraid of how I might answer. Of course, there was nothing to stop me from saying how I felt—nothing other than the time-honored Halladay tradition of keeping our emotions in check.

I had called Fred's cell phone three more times. My first two phone calls had gone unanswered. My third had gone into voice mail, where Fred's outgoing message had requested respect for the thirty-day, no-contact policy under which he'd been placed.

A no-contact policy? Had Fred gone to Paris to enter rehab for some unknown addiction? Or, in his efforts to find excitement, had he already been tossed into a Parisian jail?

I pushed another piece of meat loaf frantically across my plate, my shock and anger shifting closer and closer to full-out panic.

What on earth had he done?

I needed to find out what was going on, but how could I if he wouldn't take my calls?

My insides spiraled into a knot. I set down my fork with a loud clank, unable to take the silence for another moment. "Are we going to talk about this? Any of it?"

Five sets of eyes met mine, the expression on each family member's face one of shock, as if the idea of communicating were foreign to them.

"How about the termites? Can we talk about those?" I asked. "I planned to go over Frank Turner's estimate with Fred, but"—I laughed sharply—"that's not going to happen."

My father visibly relaxed, as if he were happy I'd limited my initial conversation to pest control. "It's a two-hundred-year-old house, Abby. You can't wait for Fred. Hire Frank."

Frank Turner had been a fixture in my hometown for as long as I could remember. As a kid, I'd called Frank "The Bug Man" in deference to the giant ant that graced the roof of his company van.

Mom nodded. "He's very fair."

"His crew can be there by nine tomorrow morning," I said.

Dad waved his fork in my direction. "I'll give him a call and take care of it."

I blew out a sigh. "Thanks," I said. I figured I might as well keep talking while we were on a problem-solving roll. "What about Fred? He does own half of the house. Shouldn't I check with him before we do any work?"

My father stared at me blankly. "He's an accountant, Abby. Profit and loss. The sooner you kill those termites, the sooner you stop the damage."

He was right, and I nodded. Then I decided to give the conversation one more push.

"His message says he's out of contact for thirty days." I arched my brows. "What do you make of that?"

"Drugs," Nan said with a hint of enjoyment. "They always go silent for thirty days when it's drugs."

I rubbed my face. "I don't think it's drugs—"

"I never liked that Fred," my father said around a mouthful of meat loaf.

"You said *yes* when 'that Fred' asked for my hand in marriage."

Another wave of his fork, this time at me. "I never said I liked him."

"Drugs," Nan repeated. "It's always the quiet ones." Then, as if all my concerns had been addressed by her comment, "Macaroon, how about a lift to the library later, since you're not doing anything?"

Nan had nicknamed me after her favorite cookie years earlier. I'd gotten used to the term of endearment. The since-you're-not-doing-anything line was a bit more difficult to swallow.

"Sure, Nan," I said, shoving down my frustration at my family's inability to have a real conversation.

"Take Bessie." My father pointed a dinner roll in my direction. "See how she handles for you."

Some families handed down heirloom watches or tea sets. My family handed down monstrous, gas-guzzling automobiles. Bessie was Dad's pride and joy, a 1968 Checker cab that had once been my grandfather's pride and joy, the building block of the Halladay Cab Company, which Grandpa Gus and my father had built into something of a legend. Dad had sold off the business and the fleet last year to a solid offer from a competitor. Unwilling to go into full retirement, however, he'd kept Bessie, making short runs most afternoons to stay busy.

Hearing him tell me to take his beloved antique cab was almost as shocking as hearing Fred say he'd jetted off to France.

Almost.

"Thanks, but I have a perfectly good car," I said.

"I'm talking about work." Dad nodded, a man of few words. "You've got a mortgage to think about now."

As if I hadn't given *that* any thought since the phone call from Max, my editor.

"You can't sit around moping," Mom singsonged. "Best to get right back up on the horse."

Frustration edged through me. "I'm a columnist, Mom, not a cattle herder."

My mother clucked her tongue and smiled. "Tone of voice, Abigail."

Frankie's entire demeanor had improved. She'd pushed aside her meat loaf and devoured her green beans, her eyes bright, attention rapt. Apparently not being the center of the familial nagging had done wonders for her mood.

I narrowed my eyes at her, and she stuck out her tongue.

Nan bit into one of my mother's rolls and gave it a good yank. Her upper partial sailed into the mashed potatoes and landed with a *splat*.

"Nan, I think you lost something, sugar," Missy drawled.

Mom reached for a napkin and the bowl of mashed potatoes simultaneously.

"Gross." Frankie groaned as she pushed away from the table and headed for the stairs.

My sister had started fleeing the dinner table sometime during her thirteenth year, and my father had long since stopped yelling at her to come back and sit down. He waved his fork at Frankie's departing backside. "What's the matter with Her Grace this time?"

Mom fished Nan's partial out of the potatoes and smiled. "Just a phase, dear. You remember Abby at the same age."

I shook my head, sliding my meat loaf into my napkin and wishing fervently, not for the first time, that my parents had a dog. "I never—"

My father held up a hand to cut me off. "I have distinct memories of bailing you out of jail."

Missy gasped and clutched a hand to her throat, doing a perfect imitation of a tiny Southern woman stricken with the vapors.

"Once." I looked at the ceiling, praying for divine intervention, a move that had yet to yield results for me.

"You did time, Abigail Marie," my mother said.

"Two hours."

Missy clucked her tongue, sounding exactly like our mother. I slumped in my chair, knowing better than to argue my case.

"Sit up straight, dear," my mother called out over her shoulder as she headed for the kitchen to rinse Nan's teeth.

I inhaled slowly through my nose and shut my eyes.

Nan pushed back from the table. "You ready to roll, Maca-roon?" she asked, her words garbled by her temporary lack of teeth.

"Absolutely." I nodded.

After all, it wasn't like I was doing anything.

CHAPTER THREE

—— —— ——

I dropped Nan at the library a little while later. She made the short walk over and back every night after dinner, claiming the library's new café made better tea than my mother, which was perfectly plausible.

While most every other building in town was Victorian and small, the Paris branch of the Hunterdon County library system was anything but. A sprawling wonder of full-wall windows, cathedral ceilings, and light, the building held a place of prominence along Race Street and attracted patrons from surrounding communities.

I suspected Nan came for the quiet. She and Grandpa used to spend their afternoons at the library together. Maybe she felt close to him here, a bit like revisiting their place for a little while each evening.

I watched until she disappeared through the front doors and then I headed for Bridge Street, turning left before the road climbed up and over the Delaware River. I parked in the municipal lot beside the river and walked across the street to the Paris Inn Pub.

I'd put in a call to Jessica Capshaw and Destiny Jones. The three of us had been friends since first grade, and if anyone could help me make sense of my day, perhaps they could. Jessica and I spoke on the phone regularly, but Destiny and I typically saw each other only when the three of us got together—which hadn't been that often during the past two years.

Not a single set of headlights came across the old suspension bridge that spanned the Delaware as I crossed the street. As a child, I'd thought the bridge monstrous, a green steel gateway to the world outside Paris. But now I laughed at my realization that the Pennsylvania side of the river was little more than a stone's throw away.

Funny how a person's perspective changes from childhood to adulthood.

I carefully navigated the narrow steps that led from the cobblestone sidewalk down to the Pub's original gated entryway. Motivated by a desire to look as if I had my act together—even though nothing felt further from the truth—I'd dressed in the classic sweater dress and chunky-heeled boots I'd planned to wear out tonight with Fred.

Paris, France.

The words taunted me and a wave of loss hit me with such force I grabbed for the wrought-iron railing and held on tight.

Two months. We were getting married in two months. How could he do this? Why would he do this?

Beside me, hitching posts still held their place from the inn's former stagecoach-stop days, and I thought about turning around, driving back to my parents' house, and hiding in my old room. But, as I pulled open the Pub's heavy wooden door, the sound of laughter and music embraced me like a long-lost friend.

All of Paris turned out to sing and laugh and drink on Wednesday nights. In high school and college, I hadn't missed a single karaoke night, but in recent years my visits had been few and far between.

A fire roared in the majestic brick hearth, and I wondered why I hadn't visited more often during the years I'd lived nearby, in Hopewell. On the rare occasion I'd convinced Fred to make the drive to meet me, we'd merely sat and watched others sing.

Manny the barber and Pete the grocer belted out the chorus to "Mack the Knife" while the rest of the patrons at the Pub's weekly karaoke night sang along.

I thought about writing my name on the sign-up sheet, suddenly craving the days when I'd participated during karaoke night, but I shook off the urge, focusing instead on finding my friends. Plus, it was a well-known reality that once the Pub's karaoke night got under way, the sign-up list was basically worthless.

I spotted Destiny sitting at the bar.

She studied me from behind her chunky black glasses as she tucked a wayward strand of purple-striped mahogany hair up under her Trenton Thunder ball cap.

"Where's Jessica?" I asked as I pulled up a stool.

"Nice to see you, too," Destiny answered, one eyebrow lifting.

"Sorry. It's just been an unbelievably bad day, and if I break down and cry…"

Destiny winced.

I pointed at her expression. "She's better than you at handling emotions."

Destiny tipped her head from side to side. "True." Then her expression grew serious. "That bad?"

I nodded.

"Well"—she held up her beer bottle in a toast—"whatever it is, you'd better pull up your big-girl panties and deal with it."

I blinked, looking around the room. Where *was* Jessica?

Destiny let loose with a belly laugh that turned every head within a ten-foot radius, yet she seemed neither to notice nor mind—an ability I'd always admired.

Destiny had once been the girl who hid from thunderstorms, but after her mother died of cancer partway through our fifth-grade year at Paris Elementary, she never hid from anything again.

While I admired her ability to live life without a safety net, I also found Destiny intimidating. I lived life via plans and to-do lists. I often wondered if we would have been friends if not for Jessica, the glue that held us together.

"She'll be here any minute," she said, as if reading my mind. "Want a drink?" She gestured to Jerry, the regular Pub bartender, who gave me a warm greeting, then poured my glass of pinot noir. I downed it in three gulps, eliciting a whistle from Destiny.

"Wow, you did have a bad day, didn't you?"

I raised my hand, catching Jerry's attention and pointing to my empty glass.

Jessica slipped into the space between us and looped her arms around our necks. "Hello, ladies."

As usual, the single mom of seven-year-old Max and five-year-old Bella looked effortlessly beautiful, tired, and happy, all at the same time.

She'd once dreamed of life outside Paris, cooking and catering her way to the top, but all that had changed when she lost her heart—and her life savings—to her first husband, a fellow chef who had promised her the world but had abandoned her instead.

With the help of her family, she'd returned to Paris and had rebuilt the Paris River Café, turning the once-empty storefront into a gathering place for good food and good people.

She slid a small pouch to Destiny, who grinned like she'd been handed a winning lottery ticket.

"Don't tell me," I groaned.

"Booty pack." Jessica gave a quick lift and drop of her shoulders. "Destiny can't make tomorrow morning's Clipper meeting, so I figured I'd let her check out my stash early."

"I can't believe you two joined the Clippers." I pointed to the pouch filled to brimming with coupons. "Why can't you call that a coupon caddy like everyone else?"

Destiny squinted one eye and spoke out of the corner of her mouth. "Argh. Where be the fun in that?"

Founded by Jessica's grandmother after she'd seen a PBS special on organizing coupon clubs, the Paris Clippers had outfitted themselves with pirate paraphernalia and embraced the art of couponing.

The shoppers of Paris had never been the same.

"Is Mona still the Clipper captain?" I asked.

Jessica smiled. "And damn proud of it." She leaned over the bar. "Could I get a water, please, Jerry? Max and Bella have a field trip tomorrow afternoon," she said, turning her focus back to us. "I can't afford a fuzzy head." She tapped the stem of my wineglass. "Why are you drinking wine?"

I sat up a bit straighter. "I like wine."

Jessica frowned. "Since when?"

Since Fred told me wine was more sophisticated than beer. "Since always."

Jessica and Destiny suddenly wore matching expressions, mixtures of disbelief and anticipation.

"Start talking," Jessica said.

And so I did. I described my day in detail, starting with the cancellation of my column and ending with Fred's completely out-of-character flight to Europe.

Neither of them said anything for several long seconds.

Jessica blew out a sigh and made a snapping noise with her mouth. "Well, that's certainly—"

"One hell of a day," Destiny finished. She pushed the booty pack across the bar to me. "You're going to need these more than I do."

I shoved them back. "I'll land another column. I just have to get some ideas together, that's all."

Destiny's brows lifted. "What about Fred?"

I slugged down another swallow of wine. "I'm sure he'll return my calls sooner or later."

Destiny scowled. "You're in denial. He hopped a plane and flew to France on the day you were supposed to start moving into your new house. He's not calling you back."

Jessica, ever the peacemaker, patted my shoulder. "I'm sure he'll call you eventually. I just wish you knew whether or not he was okay."

"Okay?" Destiny shook her head. "He's ignoring her. He's fine. The way I see it, she can either get on a plane and go after him, or she can wait it out here."

Get on a plane.

The words alone sent cold chills dancing down my spine.

"She can't get on a plane," Jessica said. "She's terrified of flying."

"I'm right here." My voice was barely audible above the sounds of karaoke night.

Manny and Pete, apparently unwilling to surrender the stage to whoever else might be waiting to perform, swung into a new number, crooning the lyrics to "New York, New York" at a pitch that would have sent dogs screaming.

"Well?" Destiny asked. "Do you want a step-by-step guide for how to fix your life or are you going to get out your notebook and start making new plans?"

I squinted at her, rubbing at the sudden dull ache in my temples. "What did you do?" I asked. "Smash your thumb with a hammer today or something?"

True to the tough-as-nails exterior Destiny had perfected, she'd forged a career as a carpenter, slowly building her custom furniture and cabinetmaking business in one of my favorite Paris buildings—a rehabbed, two-story garage tucked away on Artisan Alley, the small street that ran from the center of town down toward the river.

Her lips quirked, and for a moment I thought she might smile. I was wrong.

"So you had a shitty day," she said with a wave of her hand. "Deal with it. Call Fred and tell him to get back here if that's what you want." She leaned a bit closer. "Personally, I'd tell him to stay there." She took a long swallow of beer. "March down to the paper and give your boss an idea for a better column. Then march over to your house and figure out what you need to do to move in. You don't need us to tell you this stuff." She pointed her finger dangerously close to my nose. "And you don't need Fred."

"You never liked him," I said, feeling as though Destiny's words had sapped the last of my energy.

"Sure she did...*does*," Jessica said. "We're all just upset right now. You'll fix this. You always do."

Destiny took a long draw on her beer bottle and tipped her chin toward the far end of the bar. "Could be worse. You could be Mick."

I followed her gaze to where Mick stood, talking to Jerry.

"I don't think he's gotten the warmest welcome home," Jessica said.

"No wonder." Destiny gave a quick shrug. "People tend to remember when you burn down a landmark."

The old guilt flared to life inside me and I spoke a bit too loudly in an effort to change the subject. "Would you believe he was up on my parents' roof today? Last I heard, he was an architect out west. What's he doing replacing roof shingles in Paris?"

"He *was* an architect." Destiny leaned close and dropped her voice low. "I heard he had a great career going before his wife died."

Wife? Died?

"What are you talking about?" I tried to reconcile the happy man I'd seen today with the image of a widower.

"It just hit the grapevine this week," Jessica said. "You know those O'Malleys. They—"

"—keep to themselves," Destiny finished.

But once upon a time, Mick hadn't kept to himself. He'd told me everything.

"Well," I said, sitting back in my chair and raising my hands in the air, "the beauty of Paris is that sooner or later we'll know everything about Mick O'Malley whether he wants us to or not."

The volume inside the Pub had gone low as a new song started, and my words blasted from my lips far louder than I'd anticipated.

I glanced again at Mick, watching as he slid a bill across the bar and grabbed a six-pack to go. His gaze locked with mine in the split second it took him to turn and walk away.

Destiny slid the booty pack back in my direction. "I think there's one in here that lets you extract your foot from your mouth for free."

But I wasn't laughing. Unless Mick had drastically changed in the past thirteen years, he valued his privacy above just about everything else.

Suddenly I needed to be alone.

I said good night, slid a few bills onto the bar to cover my drinks, and headed out into the Paris night.

CHAPTER FOUR

I left my car in the municipal lot and took the long way home, letting the cool night air seep into my skin. I hoped to walk off the wine I drank far too quickly and the headache I had from my conversation with Destiny and Jessica.

I knew they meant well, but right now, I was having trouble wrapping my head around everything that had happened, let alone making plans for how to fix things.

What on earth would possess Fred to jet off across the ocean on a whim? Sensible people did not just take off for Europe, and Fred was the most sensible person I knew.

What if it hadn't been a whim? What if there was someone else? What if he planned to never come back? What if he planned to never marry me? What if he planned to spend his life searching for nonboredom along the streets of Paris, France?

I studied the pattern of octagonal cobblestones beneath my feet as I headed for the center of town. In the town square, where Bridge Street, Race Street, and Artisan Alley came together, local merchants carried on the well-loved tradition of painting their storefronts as bright as possible. Celery-green paint trimmed purple. Mustard-edged fire-engine red. Some of the oldest buildings in Paris, each had settled into angles that might make a geometry teacher proud.

I turned down Artisan Alley, halfheartedly glancing at the eclectic mix of goods lurking in the shop windows as I backtracked toward Front Street and the parking lot.

Hand-loomed rugs. Stained-glass ornaments. Antiques. Rare books.

Thanks to its quirky yet charming personality, Paris had become something of a tourist attraction in central Jersey, a location viewed by many as the perfect spot for a weekend getaway or a full-day shopping trip. It was the place where I had thought I'd spend the rest of my life. With Fred.

When I reached my car, I hesitated, but then continued to walk. The night air was doing me good, and I'd downed my two glasses of wine quickly enough that I'd rather walk the few blocks home.

At the end of Front Street, I scooted around the sign that marked the start of the bike and hike trail that ran alongside the river, and headed for Third Avenue.

The expanse of green lawn that marked the property line for the Bainbridge Estate loomed before me. Years earlier, the mansion had fallen into disrepair, becoming something of a magnet for local teens as a place to hang out and explore.

During one such "exploration," the Paris Oak, a two-hundred-year-old tree, had been burned to the ground on a cold October night. The town leaders, devastated by the loss, had placed a memorial boulder on the spot where the tree once stood.

I stared at the words "destroyed by vandals" and cringed. It could have been worse. The town council could have named names when it commissioned the rock.

I'd stood here with Fred on the day we'd toured the Bainbridge Estate in preparation for our wedding.

"Haven't you ever done anything crazy?" he'd asked, staring down at the inscription.

For a fleeting moment, I'd feared he knew the truth. But Fred had been raised in a world in which everything was black and white, profit and loss, asset and liability. He was an accountant who'd been raised by accountants who'd been raised by accountants.

In Fred's world, I was an asset. Who knew what would happen if he ever saw me as a liability?

But then he'd taken me by surprise.

"Sometimes I wish I'd studied to be a clown," he said. "Or a mime."

I'd laughed. I felt horrible as soon as I did because Fred's usually controlled features looked crushed for a fleeting instant, as if my reaction had hurt him terribly.

But then he'd laughed with me, and I realized he'd been joking.

He'd put his arm around me. "The thing I love about you is your predictability."

I had smiled on the outside, but on the inside I'd thought about a time in my life when I hadn't been predictable at all.

I pulled myself out of the past and into the present, letting Fred's words bounce through my brain.

The thing I love about you is your predictability.

At the time, I thought he'd been paying me a compliment. Now I understood that somewhere along the way, my predictability had become synonymous with "boring."

On either side of Third Avenue, carefully painted Victorians lined up one after the other, sheltered beneath a canopy of stately oaks and maples. I cut across my parents' front yard in blatant disregard of my mother's don't-walk-on-the-grass rule. I stumbled at the edge of her massive tulip garden, nicking several tulips and sending pale-pink petals fluttering to the ground.

I dropped to my knees and gathered the petals, trying fruitlessly to stick them back onto the flowers. My mother was obsessive about the garden, and the annual Paris garden competition was coming up in a few weeks.

"I have half a mind to report you to the garden club." The deep rumble of Mick's voice sent me scrambling backward, falling over my heels.

I followed the sound to the tree house he'd inherited when his family moved in next door. My throat tightened, but I forced myself to speak, my cheeks hot with embarrassment. "Mick, I'm—"

"Save it." He held up a hand from where he sat near the top of the ladder.

I walked over to the old maple tree and looked up. I craned my neck, trying to see Mick's face. I was rewarded with only a clear view of the soles of his work boots.

"I shouldn't have been talking about you."

"Why not?" He leaned over the edge of the ladder, his expression kind even after what I'd said. "Because you were doing it in front of half the town? Or because my life is none of your business?"

Nerves fisted in my chest. Since when did Mick O'Malley make me nervous? "Both, actually." I rubbed at the base of my neck. "Can I come up there?"

Silence beat for a moment before Mick answered. "I think that's the first time you've ever asked permission."

I laughed a little and nodded. He was right. I climbed onto the first rung, but my heels slipped precariously.

"Maybe you should leave the big-girl shoes down there."

At least my lack of coordination could still make Mick smile.

I pulled off my boots and climbed barefoot, wrapping my toes around each rung, concentrating on moving slowly, hand over hand, foot over foot. When Mick's fingers wrapped around my wrist, relief washed through me.

I climbed up onto the rough wood floor and sank to my knees, a bit breathless from the climb and from being face-to-face with Mick in the place where so much of our youth had played out.

Ancient handwritten signs and posters clung to the walls, their corners peeling, faded memories of the bond we'd shared long ago.

Mick took a long draw on a beer, then slid the six-pack toward me. I shook my head. It had been a long time since I'd had a good, cold beer, but the last thing I needed was one more thing to mess with my senses.

We'd sat in the spot countless times before, yet this time the atmosphere between us felt anything but comfortable. We were strangers now. Adults. Neither of us knew much of anything about the other or the type of person we'd each become.

Mick slid his empty bottle into the sleeve of the six-pack and leaned back on his elbows. "Aren't you going to ask?"

I pretended I had no idea what he was talking about. "About what?"

He laughed. "You're a horrible liar."

"So I hear." I studied my hands, folded in my lap.

"How much do you know?" he asked.

I moved to the side of the tree house and let my legs dangle over the edge. The cool night air brushed against my skin and reminded me of how simple life had once been. "I know you were married."

He moved beside me, leaving only a few inches of space between us. His jean-clad legs swung in a rhythm matching my own.

"I never knew that before tonight," I said. "But then, you were never the let's-send-out-an-announcement sort of guy."

The corner of his mouth lifted. "No."

I studied the sharp line of his jaw, the tired set of his eyes, and the creases bracketing his features. "What was her name?"

"Mary." He spoke the word softly, as if he'd gone far away inside his mind.

"What happened?"

"She drove drunk."

My mind flew to another night. A single car accident. A beat-up sedan wrapped around a tree. The night Mick's dad had died.

"We'd been arguing. I should have taken her keys," he said.

"You let her drive drunk?" I hated myself as soon as I spoke the words.

Mick turned to face me, his expression pained. "She hadn't been drinking the last time I saw her."

"What do you mean?"

"I should have known better." He focused on a point in the sky above his mother's house.

In a town as small as Paris, Ed O'Malley's drinking hadn't been a secret. Nor had it been a topic about which folks stayed quiet out of respect. No. Ed O'Malley's drinking had been fair game. And as the Paris gossips dragged Ed through their mud, they'd dragged Mick and his mother, Detta, along behind him. Guilt by association.

Mick, true to form, had lived up to expectations, being something of a bad boy at school, spending more time in the principal's office than he spent in class.

But I knew differently. I'd known Mick better than most anyone else in Paris.

Mick hated being the son of the town drunk, and once he'd had an excuse to leave, he'd done just that.

"He wasn't drunk the night he died," Mick said, his thoughts having apparently followed a path similar to mine.

My mind swirled with confusion. But I said nothing. I waited for Mick to talk.

He let go of a bitter laugh. "He did most everything else under the influence, but he never got the behind the wheel of that car if he'd had so much as a drop."

"I don't understand," I said.

Mick reached for the six-pack and pulled the bottles close. "Hitting that tree was the only sober decision he ever made." He twisted off the five remaining caps. "Sure you don't want one?"

I nodded numbly, working to absorb what Mick had just said. I reached for his arm, letting my fingers brush against his jacket before pulling away.

Mick poured beer down onto the lawn, one bottle at a time, until the remaining five were empty. He lined them into a single row, then returned each to the carrier.

I frowned, my head beginning to pound. "Why did you do that?" I asked, even though I knew exactly why Mick had done what he did. He wanted to be nothing like his father, even though he'd tried to please the man for as long as I knew him.

Mick shrugged. "It's just something I do."

The moon cast a bluish glow, lighting Mick's face and shadowing his eyes.

"How long ago did she die?" I asked.

"Two years last month."

"Why didn't you come home after it happened?"

"I was home."

"In Seattle?"

Mick nodded.

"What about Paris?"

"I didn't need Paris," he answered.

"Didn't need it, or didn't want it?"

He turned to face me, and I spied the traces of the teenager I'd once known. Tough on the outside, scared to death on the inside. "Is there a difference?"

I fought the urge to lean against him, to close the gap of space and time the years had put between us. Instead, I looked up at the sky, amazed, as always, at the sheer number of stars visible in the night sky above my hometown.

"Do you remember how many nights we sat here trying to count the stars?" I asked.

I looked at Mick and he smiled, ever so slightly. "I never tried to count them."

"But you sat here with me while I did."

His smile fell. "That was a long time ago, Abby."

I looked down at my dress and smoothed an invisible wrinkle.

"Do you still count them?" he asked.

"No," I answered, suddenly wondering when it was that I'd stopped.

"That's too bad," Mick said.

Melancholy twisted inside me. I needed to get home before the wine and the night and the thought of Fred ditching me like yesterday's news swallowed me whole.

I scrambled toward the ladder. "I need to go." I hesitated as I backed toward the top rung. "Sorry again about tonight."

Our gazes locked and something flashed in Mick's eyes. I wasn't sure if he was angry or sad. "Next time, come to me instead of the town gossips," he said.

"Those gossips are my friends."

He nodded. "I know."

A few minutes later, I crawled beneath the covers in my old bedroom. Someone had fixed the slats on my bed and opened the curtains to let the moonlight spill through the glass panes.

I stared at the window for a long while, wondering what other secrets Mick's life held. I reminded myself that Mick's life was none of my business.

I shifted my gaze to the ceiling, where the stars shimmered as brilliantly as I remembered.

For a brief moment, I thought about counting them, but then my heartache and emotions and memories crashed into a tangled mess that knotted my gut and hurt my brain.

So, instead of gazing at the brilliance of the stars above me, I simply closed my eyes and fell asleep.

CHAPTER FIVE

— — —

I floated down the Seine on a riverboat tour, a loaf of crusty bread and a dry pinot noir by my side. Suddenly, the riverboat shapeshifted into a gondola, steered by a single figure expertly wielding his oar as he guided us down a narrow canal.

I sat up and set down my bread. "I've got a feeling we're not in Paris anymore."

The gondolier turned toward me, his face nothing more than a featureless mask. He lifted his oar clear of the water's current and stepped toward me, raising his oar menacingly.

When he gave me a swift thwack over the head, I scrambled toward the opposite end of the boat. He came at me a second time, and I fought to shake myself from the dream.

History showed me that my dreams were typically neither soothing nor geographically accurate. Yet, even for the French, I thought this particular dream a bit rude. Of course, most everyone in France, especially Fred, was not terribly high on my "like" list at the moment.

The man's face faded before my eyes, and I blinked against the cruel glare of morning light. A horrific banging, however, persisted. Even though I knew the noise originated from somewhere outside my bedroom, the ensuing pain was no less intense than if the hammering were inside my brain.

I shielded my eyes against the brightness of daylight, threw a robe over my T-shirt and shorts, and shoved up the window sash.

I peered outside my opened window and frowned.

Rat tat tat. Mick bent over the roof, all good-morning focus and masculine brawn. *Rat tat tat.*

He effortlessly hammered nails into the black roof wrap, sending shockwaves of pain through my gray matter.

"Mick—" My voice sounded more like a two-hundred-year-old frog than a thirty-year-old female. I cleared my throat to try again "Mick! Are you kidding me?"

He lifted his gaze just high enough to meet mine. Amusement played beneath his Seattle Mariners cap, and my insides twisted.

Our conversation from the night before ran through my mind, and my heart hurt for all he'd endured.

"Seriously, what are you doing?" I asked.

He grinned. "Good morning. How did you sleep? Beautiful day, isn't it? Nice work. Would you like a cup of coffee?"

Rat tat tat.

"Social skills, Halladay. Or did your manners skip to Paris along with your fiancé?"

So he knew. Not that I was surprised.

"No secrets in this town," I said, working to ignore the pain in my head and my heart.

"None." *Rat tat tat.* "Maybe I'm just jealous your stunning beauty's been wasted on someone else."

I reached my hands up to my hair, doing my best to smooth the snarled strands. "Maybe I wouldn't look so scary if I'd gotten more sleep."

He arched his dark brows and laughed. "Not likely." *Rat tat tat.* "I waited until nine thirty. Some of us have jobs to finish."

Nine thirty?

I pushed away from the window and pressed a button on my cell phone. Nine thirty.

I groaned.

I'd wanted to be on-site when Frank Turner and his crew started work at nine o'clock. So much for my ability to keep myself on track.

I stuck my head back out the window, already fantasizing about an afternoon nap. "You'll be gone later, right?"

Rat tat tat. "Social skills, Halladay." *Rat tat tat.* "Social skills."

I shut the window, drew the curtains, and tossed my suitcase on the bed. I traded my shorts for a pair of jeans, tossed my robe on a chair, and pulled a rumpled sweater over my T-shirt. I glanced in the mirror, smoothed the front of my sweater, and thought about brushing my hair. I chose my Trenton Thunder ball cap instead and tucked my tangled mess up under the navy rim.

I raced downstairs, reaching the hallway credenza in record time. When I reached for the clover-shaped dish where I typically left my keys whenever I visited my parents' house, I remembered one crucial detail.

I'd left my car in the municipal lot and walked home from the inn.

"Mom?" I called out. "Can I borrow the car?"

My mother insisted on owning one nontaxi vehicle in case of emergency.

This was an emergency.

"Nan took it to Clippers, honey."

Apparently *that* had been a bigger emergency. Nan, who refused to drive at night, had been known to motor about town all day long. She'd once tried to hijack Bessie, my dad's cab. He'd made it clear the classic car was off-limits.

Along with my mother's voice, a heavenly smell wafted down the hall from the kitchen. Madeline Halladay might be incapable of making an edible dinner, but she was an amazing baker, a bit like those prodigies who failed miserably in math but played professional violin by age four.

Drawn to the potent combination of yeast, cinnamon, and nutmeg, I headed for the kitchen, forcing myself to remain focused on getting to my meeting.

If Nan had taken the car to the Clippers, I'd have to walk... quickly. My head pounded at the thought. Then I thought of the more obvious solution.

At the kitchen counter, my mother gingerly lifted muffins from a baking pan while Missy sat at the kitchen table, a rainbow of crayons spread before her as she created a masterpiece on construction paper.

"Morning," I said.

"Morning, sweetheart," my mom answered.

"Morning," Missy mumbled without looking up, deep in concentration. I couldn't help but notice the Southern accent had gone missing.

"Where's Dad?" I asked.

"He took your bike out for a ride."

I frowned. There were several words in my mother's sentence that didn't add up. Bike. Out. Ride.

"My bike?" I asked.

Mom nodded.

"My pink bike?"

41

She nodded again.

"Do you know where he went?" I asked.

"No," my mother answered without looking up.

"He goes every day," Missy volunteered, adding a splash of orange to the sunburst in the upper right corner of her drawing.

My mother pretended to concentrate on arranging muffins on her china platter.

"You don't know where he goes?" I repeated.

My mother pursed her lips and shook her head. "No."

"Don't you care?"

She gave a slight shrug of her slender shoulders. "If your father wants to get in shape, Abigail, that's his business." The woman was either in denial or the best actress I'd ever seen.

I, for one, didn't believe a word. My mother had made an annoyed facial expression *and* shrugged, all in the span of ten seconds. She might be poised on the outside, but on the inside, she was dying to know where Dad went.

"Why didn't you ask him?" I asked.

"He's partially retired, dear. He's allowed to ride a bike." Then she pivoted toward me. "Muffin?"

The woman always had known how to throw a distraction.

"Your father left you Bessie," she said, reaching for a napkin to wrap around my breakfast. "He wants you to drive by the café when the Clippers let out. You might get lucky and pick up a few fares, depending on how anxious everyone is to get shopping."

"I'm a writer, Mom. I am not driving that cab." I jerked my thumb toward the kitchen window, through which the cab was visible, sitting out back on a custom asphalt pad beneath a custom-made UV-protective tent.

"You'd better get a move on. There's no way Frank Turner is going to wait more than forty-five minutes for you."

You had to hand it to the woman. She was good. Not only could she avoid talking about topics she chose not to talk about, but she could leave you thinking the decision to walk away had been your own.

"Okay." I reached for the hallowed keys. "But only because I need a ride."

"Have a nice day, dear." Mom reconsidered the muffins and handed me two. "Don't forget about the Clippers."

"Clippers," I muttered beneath my breath. "This whole town's gone a little Clipper crazy."

Missy sprang out of her chair, landed in the middle of the kitchen floor, and broke into an elaborate song and dance. "I'm a Clipper. She's a Clipper. Wouldn't you like to be a Clipper, too?" She threw out her arms, ending her brief routine with a flourish.

Mom and I applauded. "Your sister saw an old Dr Pepper commercial on the Internet this morning," she said.

Then she leaned close to me and spoke softly. "I think our Southern belle days may be gone with the wind."

"Well, I'll miss her," I said, "but this new routine is something else."

Missy beamed and took a deep bow.

I headed out to Checker cab central and climbed inside the Beast, as I liked to call good old Bessie. Immaculate as always, her wood paneling gleamed. Somewhere along the way, Dad had wrapped the steering wheel in leather.

I turned the key in the ignition, amazed at how smooth the car sounded.

My father loved this automobile, and it showed.

I reached for the pedal to release the parking brake and pulled on the old-fashioned gearshift, crossing my fingers I'd shifted correctly.

Dad had taught me how to drive on Bessie. While I hadn't appreciated his efforts at the time, I did now. The way I saw it, if I could drive Bessie, I could drive just about anything.

I maneuvered the huge car down the driveway and out onto Third Avenue. I headed left on Front Street, driving well below the speed limit. My every muscle tensed; I feared I'd misjudge the Beast's girth and sideswipe another car…a bike rider…a building.

I took a left on Bridge Street and another quick left on Stone Lane, a sense of dread building inside me. Second Avenue loomed on my right and I braked to let an orange cat cross my path before I took the turn. With any luck at all, Frank Turner would have good termite news for me, if there were such a thing.

I pulled the Beast to the curb, cut the ignition, and made my way up the center walk. Frank was nowhere in sight, but I found his crew near the back section of the porch, preparing to drill the foundation of the house.

"He left," said Barney, Frank's right-hand man.

I swallowed my sigh, knowing an apology was in order. "I'm sorry I'm late. Can you reach him on the phone for me, at least?"

"He asked not to be disturbed," Barney explained. "Important meeting."

"Another client?" I asked.

He shook his head. "Clippers. He said you could meet him over at the café, but don't interrupt the Booty Bonanza. It's Frank's week to pull the winning numbers."

I fought the urge to roll my eyes. "Booty Bonanza, got it. I'll be able to move back in later today, right?"

Barney's features turned serious and he shook his head.

"Damage?" I asked.

Barney nodded. "Major. But he wants to tell you himself."

My left eye twitched again. This time I did nothing to hide the offending lid.

Barney winced. "Try to act surprised."

"Act surprised," I repeated.

Not a problem.

CHAPTER SIX

A warm mix of rich and buttery scents wrapped around me as I stepped into the Paris Café. Even more than the scents of Jessica's restaurant, it was the ambiance that made me feel at home whenever I stopped by. I loved the laughter, the animated talk, the camaraderie that filled the air.

Most of Paris considered Jessica's a home away from home. Never was that more evident than right now.

The café buzzed with activity. Families gathered. Couples talked. And the Clippers congregated in the back half of the dining room.

"Argh, argh, argh," Mona Capshaw cried out. No less than thirty other so-called adults answered, "Argh. Argh. Argh."

Jessica stood behind the gleaming breakfast counter and poured a mug of her to-die-for coffee. She grinned as she slid the mug in my direction. "Have you seen the error of your non-clipping ways?"

I gave a tight shake of my head. "Looking for Frank."

She pointed toward the far wall. "Careful. He's on his third cup, and I'm not pouring decaf."

Super. Frank Turner was a fast talker—a ridiculously fast talker. I had trouble understanding the man when he *wasn't* hyped up on Jessica's famous high-test brew.

I headed for the group of tables where the Clippers had spread their loot. The frenzy had begun. Members exchanged sale flyers and cut coupons with dizzying efficiency.

I waved to Frank, but he shook his head, his eyebrows pulling together.

"Time for the Booty Bonanza," Mona called out.

I reached Frank's table just as Mona handed him a jar full of red tickets.

"Not now, Abby," he said. "It's my week to call the numbers."

"But this will only take a minute."

"Step aside, landlubber," Mona said.

I thought about shooting Jessica's grandmother my best death glare, but instead I leaned down close to Frank and dropped my voice. "If you could just bring me up to speed on the damage, I'll—"

"I heard it's major," said Polly Perkins, owner of the Paris Clip and Curl.

"That's what I wanted to talk to Frank—"

Ted Miller, town pharmacist and the guy who had taken me to my first homecoming dance, interrupted me. "I heard they canceled your column."

"That's just a temporary setback. I'm sure I'll—"

"I heard that accountant boyfriend of yours left town," Mona chimed in.

"I heard he left the country." Frank made a *tsk*ing noise as he readied to pull the winning bonanza tickets.

I pulled my cap a bit lower over my face and threw back a mouthful of Jessica's brew to fortify myself. I stepped away from Frank. "Maybe you could just give me a call later on."

Jessica anchored her arm around my shoulders and steered me away from the group.

"I think I hate those Clippers," I muttered.

She bit back a laugh. "Now, you know they have your best interests at heart."

"I don't see how you can say that with a straight face."

She spun me toward the door. "Sorry to hear about your house. Any word from Fred?"

I shook my head.

Jessica tightened her grip on my shoulder, her features going serious. "Did you ever stop to think you didn't give him much of a choice about living in Paris?"

"Choice? I didn't know anything about it."

Jessica shook her head. "Not Paris, France. Paris, *New Jersey*. Did you really give him a choice?"

I knew she was speaking from experience, having been dragged down to Atlanta as part of her first husband's scheme. Things between Fred and me had been different, though.

"We had a plan," I said.

Fred and I had picked Paris as the midpoint between our jobs, found a house we loved, and paid a below-market purchase price. On the ledger sheet of life, our plan made sense.

Jessica searched my gaze, her eyes softening. "You had a plan. Are you sure Fred did?"

I drew in a slow breath, letting her question sink in. Truth was, I couldn't answer her.

"I'm going for a drive." I handed her back the oversize coffee mug. "I'll call you later."

The morning had turned a bit breezy by the time I fled the Clipper meeting. The sky had darkened, and storm clouds swirled to the west of town.

I headed back toward my parents' house, not knowing where else to go.

A few pedestrians waved as I maneuvered Bessie through the streets of Paris. I waved back, buoyed by the kindness pervasive in Paris. Whether or not Fred came back, I was staying. Where else would people go so far out of their way to wave to you?

I paused for a stop sign, glancing down at the polished wood dashboard and the gleaming trip meter box. Then I remembered the taxi sign on the roof of the car.

The friendly pedestrians hadn't waved out of the goodness of their hearts. They'd wanted a lift to their destinations before the impending storm hit.

A smattering of raindrops hit the windshield, stopping as quickly as they'd started. Thank goodness. I had no idea which button turned on the Beast's windshield wipers.

I glanced down at the grouping of buttons to the left of the steering wheel and frowned. I refocused on the road just in time to see an elderly woman step off the curb directly in front of me. Slamming on the ancient brakes, I silently thanked God when the cab stopped without plowing the woman down.

She wore only a thin housedress and a pair of slippers as she bent alongside the curb, lifting what appeared to be a very dead houseplant from a pile of trash waiting for the weekly pickup.

The woman looked up at me, her stare a bit vacant, a bit lost.

Mick's mom—Mrs. O'Malley. I'd recognize her anywhere, even if she'd obviously lost weight and seemed to be a bit confused.

I waved and smiled. Mrs. O'Malley waved back, then cradled the dead spider plant in her arm, climbed back to the sidewalk, and began walking away.

Raindrops hit the windshield once more, this time a bit harder and without any signs of letting up.

I pulled close to the sidewalk, shifted the car into Park and reached to crank down the passenger window. "Mrs. O'Malley. It's Abby Halladay. Can I give you a lift home?"

Mick's mother slowed to a stop, tightening her grip on the dead plant. The rain picked up in intensity, and brown tendrils of leaves and stems spilled over her arms. A shriveled leaf broke free, fluttering to the cobblestone path beneath her feet.

"Mrs. O'Malley?"

She looked at me then, her brow furrowed as if trying to place me. "Shouldn't you be in school?" she asked.

"No, ma'am." I smiled. "I graduated years ago. I went to school with Mick."

The older woman's frown gave way to a smile, the skin around her eyes softening, her entire countenance shifting to one of warmth. "He's a good boy, my Mick."

I climbed from the cab and slowly walked to where she stood. "Yes, he is."

"Did you know he's going to be an architect?" she asked.

I nodded, reaching out my hand. She'd grown frailer since I'd seen her last. I thought back fondly to the days when she'd climbed the ladder to the tree house to bring Mick and me freshly baked cookies or tall, cool glasses of milk. She'd had a smile that could brighten even the darkest corners of a room, and her fiery auburn hair had been the envy of every woman in Paris.

She'd gone to high school with my mother, graduating just a few years ahead, but as I took in the set of her shoulders and the paleness of her skin, Detta O'Malley seemed a decade older than I knew her to be.

I slipped out of my sweater and draped it around her shoulders. When I took her arm in mine, my heart caught at the feel of her bony elbow beneath my fingertips.

She turned to study me, her faded blue gaze searching my face. "Do I know you?"

"Abby Halladay, Mrs. O'Malley. Madeline and Buddy's girl." I steadied her as I turned her toward the cab. "Mick's friend."

"He's a good boy, my Mick." She walked beside me now, more easily led than I would have imagined. "Did you know he's going to be an architect?"

"Yes, ma'am," I said, as sadness bubbled up inside me. So this was why Mick had come home. After years of staying as far away from Paris as he could, he'd come back to take care of his mother. And though I suppose that should have surprised me on some level, it didn't.

At the core of who he was, one thing had always held true about Mick. He had a heart of gold, even if he did his best to hide it.

I helped Mrs. O'Malley settle into the passenger seat and fastened her lap belt. She held the plant and its crinkled tendrils out of the way.

"Should I put the plant in the back?" I asked.

Detta shook her head fiercely. "She needs me."

I searched the plant for a sign of life but found none.

"How could someone throw her out?" Mrs. O'Malley asked. "It's not her time."

"No, ma'am."

I didn't know what to do or say, but I thought of all the kindnesses Mrs. O'Malley had shown me through the years. Even though theirs had not been a happy home, Mick's mother had always made time to talk, to listen, to act as official scorekeeper during badminton tournaments and bike races.

Her caring presence had once been a constant in my world. I wasn't surprised she wanted to save this seemingly unsalvageable plant. Not surprised at all.

I climbed back into the driver's seat, anchored my own seat belt, turned on the wipers, and pulled the ancient gearshift into drive.

I glanced at Mrs. O'Malley and frowned. She tugged and pulled at the seat belt strap, her features twisted with frustration. "Would you like to hear some music?" I asked, searching for something I could offer to soothe her agitated state.

My father, never one to be far from his tunes, had outfitted the classic Checker with a modern CD deck. I waited for Mrs. O'Malley's nod before I pushed the power button.

"Let's see what we've got," I said, as I pushed Play.

The Mamas and the Papas sang loud and clear, filling the air inside the Beast with their amazing harmonies. Beside me, Mrs. O'Malley shifted in her seat, loosening her grip on the dead plant.

She began to sing, her voice and words spot-on with the music, matching the CD word for word and tone for tone. Her voice rang out, crystal clear and bright.

A sudden rush of memories hit me, grabbing hold of my emotions and holding tight. Summer nights with the windows open, hearing Mrs. O'Malley singing from the kitchen next door as she finished dinner. Spring mornings, watching her plant fresh annuals, softly singing all the while.

Dream a little dream of me.

Detta O'Malley loved music. Her features came to life as she sat in Dad's cab. Her eyes widened and she smiled as if the weight of the world had been lifted from her shoulders. I realized how glad I was I'd been able to offer her a ride.

My only regret was that we reached our destination before the end of the song. Maybe next time I'd drive until her voice ran dry.

She smiled—a smile that stole my breath with its palpable joy. "I knew the words," she said on an exhaled breath.

As I helped her out of the car, Mick appeared at the front door. He pressed his cell phone to his ear and spoke rapidly, keeping his voice low. "She's here now. Sorry to have bothered you."

He pressed a kiss to his mother's cheek, then looked at me, the question hanging between us, unspoken.

"I saw your mom walking in the rain after I left the Clipper meeting." I held his mother's elbow as she climbed the bottom step, afraid she might stumble. "Isn't that right, Mrs. O'Malley?"

Detta nodded. "I knew the words."

Mick's eyebrows lifted.

"To a song in the car," I answered.

His curiosity morphed to surprise; then he smiled, a luminous grin full of gratitude.

"Thank you," he said. "She loves to sing." He reached for the plant I held. "I'll take that."

I shook my head. "I've got it."

But Mick had already anchored his fingers on the edge of the tired and unwanted pot. "Thanks for bringing her home."

I'd been dismissed, and even though it had been years, I understood Mick perfectly. His family had always kept to themselves. Why should this moment be any different?

"My pleasure." I took a backward step. "I'd better get Bessie back to my dad before he sends out a search party. Great to see you, Mrs. O'Malley. See you later, Mick."

The light I'd glimpsed so briefly had already faded from Detta O'Malley's eyes. She looked at me without emotion. "Do you know my Mick?"

"Yes, ma'am." Sadness filled me at the realization she'd probably also forgotten how the music had brought her back to life. "He's a good boy."

I had Bessie parked under her tent a few minutes later, but I couldn't bring myself to go inside my parents' house to face my new, not-so-planned life. Instead I turned on Dad's CD and listened to the song Detta O'Malley had just sung.

She might not be able to remember the beautiful sound of her voice, but I could. I hoped I'd never forget the joy on her face and the power of what she'd said.

I knew the words.

But for Mrs. O'Malley, the words and music were already gone.

Suddenly my house, my job, and my engagement were merely obstacles to be overcome. I could fix my problems, but Mrs. O'Malley's life had been forever altered. Her fading memory was slowly erasing the person she'd once been.

My life had merely taken a detour—one I could handle.

As I sat inside the Beast—windows shut to the world, music blaring—I realized two things.

Driving Bessie wasn't half bad, and listening to Mrs. O'Malley sing was the most magical thing I'd witnessed in a long, long time.

CHAPTER SEVEN

— — —

Several minutes later, I sneaked in the back door and up to my old bedroom to try Fred's number again.

We sometimes went a full day without speaking to each other, but the fact he'd fled across the ocean and declared a thirty-day lockout filled me with a sense of urgency about reaching him.

"Fred," I said as soon as his outgoing message ended, "I am going to call you until you call me back. Grown people do not take off on a plane on a whim. Grown people stick to their plans...their wedding plans...their wedding plans complete with nonrefundable deposits."

Frustration and anger tangled inside me. How could we work this out if the man wouldn't pick up his phone?

"I understand you're feeling bored. Maybe I'm bored, too."

It was true, I realized. At some point, Fred and I had started watching life instead of living it.

We were boring.

"I'm ready to join the exciting team, honey. Come home and we'll take this Paris by storm...together. I love you. Call me back."

I disconnected the call and tucked my phone into the pocket of my jeans, just in case.

I crossed to the window and stared out at the roof. Mick's work sat complete—shingles patched, restored, renewed, my parents' home safe from the elements.

A bell sounded from downstairs and I resisted the urge to bang my head against the wall. My mother had been ringing a dinner bell for as long as I could remember, and while there was nothing wrong with doing so, wasn't it easier to raise your voice and holler?

I glanced in the mirror, took off my ball cap, and grimaced. At some point during the day, a shower would have been genius.

I smoothed my hair, tucked as many flat strands as I could behind my ears, and smacked my cheeks, hoping to put some color back into my tired complexion.

When I neared the bottom of the steps, I picked up threads of a conversation that included not one, but two male voices. Of all the days to invite company for dinner, Mom had to pick this one. I rounded the corner and spotted Ted Miller, town pharmacist, sitting at the dining room table with Dad.

I nodded a greeting and made a beeline for the kitchen. My mother stood at the counter, her pink-and-yellow sheath flawless and classic. I glanced down at my jeans and sweatshirt and wondered how none of her fashion sense had made its way to me. Based on the look in her eyes, she wondered the same thing.

I moved close as she refocused on placing overcooked pork chops and mushy-looking apples on a serving platter. "Why is Ted Miller here?" I asked.

"You're not getting any younger, Abby," she answered without looking up. "It's time to move on with your life."

I blinked and took a backward step.

"Move on with my life?" I whispered loudly.

"You can't sit around and mope forever."

"Fred's been gone for twenty-four hours. Don't you think you're rushing things a bit?"

"I want you to consider your options." She paused dramatically. "Ted is an option."

An option I'd never consider in a million years. Sure, Ted had taken me to my first formal dance, but to the best of my memory, the entire night had been a disaster from start to finish. He might be an upstanding citizen and a solid businessman, but there was no way I'd ever consider dating Ted Miller. Not ever.

There was also the minor detail of the fact I was supposed to be marrying Fred in two months.

"Mom, you may be overreacting to recent events."

She turned to face me, one perfect blond brow arched. "Am I?"

I certainly hoped she was, but long ago, I'd adopted the path of least resistance when it came to dealings with my mom. I saw no reason to change that now.

I drew in a deep breath and nodded. "All right. I'll be polite during dinner, but you have to promise me you won't do this again."

She smiled the same smile she'd been giving me since the first time I'd uttered the word *no*. It was the sort of smile that said, *Look how cute you are, thinking you can win.*

She reached for the faucet, running her fingers beneath a stream of water before she grabbed my head to fluff and scrunch my hair. "Much better."

She pointed over my shoulder to where a long-sleeved, pink-and-purple floral sheath hung on the powder room door.

"Go slip into that, dear. Those jeans could walk off by themselves. And use the perfume I left on the counter."

"Mom, I am not going to change clothes for Ted Miller."

"Yes, you are."

"No, I'm not."

"Yes…you *are*."

"Okay," I said as I headed for the dress and the perfume.

Five minutes later, I was changed, moisturized, spritzed, and freshened. I glanced at myself in the mirror and wondered if this was my mother's idea of who I should be. Was this the image of the daughter she wanted? Was this the image of the woman Fred wanted, as well?

More important, was this the image of me I wanted?

I glanced longingly at my jeans and sweatshirt puddled in a heap on the floor.

"Dinner, honey," Mom said, tapping softly at the door.

I shook off my thoughts of inadequacy and stepped out of the bathroom, heading for the dining room.

Mom clasped her hands together and smiled—a sure sign of approval—as I cleared the archway. The rest of the family, however, was less than enthusiastic.

"You look like Mommy," Missy said.

"I liked the hat better," Frankie grumbled.

"Not your style, Macaroon." Nan tipped her head toward my mother and grinned.

"I thought we were never going to eat," Dad said.

Ted stood up, then grabbed his calf, making it difficult to tell if he was being a gentleman or suffering a charley horse.

"Cramp." He grimaced, answering my question. "Just part of the price we pharmacists pay daily."

I managed not to roll my eyes as I took my seat. Ted sat back down, and my mother passed him the platter of pork.

"You didn't have to go to any special effort for me, Abby," he said as he filled his plate.

I was dying to say my costume change wasn't for him, but that wouldn't have been nice.

Ted, on the other hand, decided to pick up right where he'd left off at the Clipper meeting.

"I guess it was only a matter of time before that column of yours got canned."

My mother choked on her wine, and Nan kicked me beneath the table.

Every muscle in my body stiffened. "What do you mean, Ted?" I asked, in what I thought was an amazingly calm tone.

Ted shoved a forkful of pork into his mouth before he answered.

I watched his reaction carefully, knowing pork chops were not one of my mother's specialties. Honestly, no dinner was her specialty.

Ted sputtered and chewed. Then he maneuvered his food into one cheek and spoke. "Little dry tonight, Madeline. Maybe you spent too much time dressing Abby."

A stunned hush fell across the table. If there was one unspoken rule in our house, it was this. We did not speak negatively about Mom's cooking skills. Ever.

I had to shift topics…and fast.

"I'd like to hear more about your thoughts on my column, Ted," I said. If anyone was going under the bus, it might as well be me.

He put his napkin to his mouth and wiped. I knew what he was doing. The good old let's-get-rid-of-the-food maneuver. He couldn't fool me…or Mom.

She smiled, having known Ted long enough to understand he lacked the filter most of us had in social situations. I, on the other hand, longed to tell Ted exactly what I thought of his behavior, even though I said nothing.

He launched into a diatribe on the merits of logic over emotions, and how the former served a person far better than the latter ever could.

"That was the downfall of your column, Abby. Emotions. No one agrees on emotions." He waved a fork in my direction. "Now, logic and science? Everyone can agree on them because they're based on facts." Another wave of the fork. "That's your column. Go back to your boss with that idea, and he'll have you syndicated again in no time."

"Science?" I repeated, wishing Ted would either choke or chew and spit faster in order to end this dinner more quickly.

"Science." He nodded with apparent self-satisfaction. "And logic."

Most everyone in my family seemed to tune Ted out for the remainder of dinner. Nan and Dad nodded absentmindedly as they focused on eating around their pork. Frankie escaped to her room, as was her habit. Missy politely maintained eye contact as Ted blathered on for what seemed like hours.

As for me, I focused on only one thing. Sooner or later, even Ted would be tired of hearing himself talk.

CHAPTER EIGHT

— —— —

I drove Nan to the library again not long after we got rid of Ted. My mother had promised she'd try harder the next time she invited someone to dinner, even though I assured her I didn't need a next time.

Frankie had remained isolated in her room, opting not to come back downstairs for dessert.

I tried to remember if I'd done the same thing at her age, but all I could envision were evenings spent sneaking out to meet Jessica and Destiny. There had also been a time when the twilight hours post-dinnertime were spent up in the tree house, legs swinging over the side, telling Mick my dreams and schemes and counting stars.

My, how times had changed.

"Thanks for the lift, Macaroon," Nan said as I slowed the Beast to a stop in front of the library.

"Why the library?" I asked.

I expected my grandmother to tell me she enjoyed being surrounded by books, or that she met other local widows and widowers here. I expected her to tell me she went there for the tea, but instead she said, "Memories, dear."

Then she patted my hand and deftly shifted the conversation to me. "What are you going to do?"

"About what? Fred? A job? The house?"

Frank Turner had called to tell me that the structural damage to the Victorian was major, and that it was unsafe for me to move in until the first floor could be secured or restored.

For the time being, I'd be living at home with the Halladays.

Nan leaned across the wide bench seat and grasped my knee. "If I were you, I'd drive this cab, take care of your house, and let that Fred sort himself out."

Confusion swirled inside me. "Aren't you the one always touting the wonders of true love?"

"Yes." She nodded. "*True* love is a magical thing."

Nan and my grandfather had been married fifty-two years before the stroke that claimed Gus Halladay's life hit. His sudden death sent our family reeling, but Nan seemed to bounce back instantly. During the past six years, she hadn't missed a single Paris Seniors trip or dance or nightly visit to the library.

I often wondered if she kept her schedule full in the hopes of finding a new soul mate, or in the hopes of avoiding her grief.

"Abby?" Her voice jarred me from my thoughts. "You never answered my question," she said.

"Question?" Suddenly, I couldn't seem to hold a thought in my head.

"What are you going to do?" She repeated her words slowly and firmly, as if I were once again six years old.

I blinked. "I'm going after Fred." I tamped down the voice inside me that wondered how in the heck I was going to do that. "That's my top priority." I nodded, searching for approval in Nan's eyes but finding none.

Nan sank back against the plush leather seat, her lips pressed to a thin line. I leaned to kiss her cheek as she slid toward her door.

Just before she slammed the massive door shut, I could have sworn I heard her say, "That's what I was afraid of."

I scooted across the seat to roll down the window, suddenly filled with sadness at the idea of my grandmother sitting alone in the library every night with only her memories and a cup of Earl Grey.

"Do you want some company?" I called to her.

She slowed and turned, a warm smile gliding across her lips. "Thank you, dear, but not tonight. Go find some fun."

I watched until she disappeared beyond the sliding glass entry doors of the Paris Public Library.

Find some fun.

There seemed to be a theme developing along those lines.

I pulled the Beast away from the curb but then slowed to a stop a short distance down the street.

As I stared at the parked cars, I remembered my own Beetle, still sitting in the municipal lot near the inn. The least I could do would be to drive by to check on the poor thing.

I thought again of Nan and the idea of her sitting alone night after night. I glanced back at the library just in time to spot a familiar shape at the entrance.

Nan reemerged, carrying a disposable hot beverage cup. Her steps were sure and solid, as if she'd done this countless times before. She headed down the center walk and turned left, away from where I sat parked.

I pulled the Beast into an open parking space, cut the ignition, and climbed out. I moved quickly, trailing behind Nan but staying far enough back that I could duck and hide should she suddenly spin around to check for a tail.

I might be leading a boring life, but my imagination hadn't lost a step.

I glanced down at the colorful sheath in which my mother had dressed me and realized I could duck all I wanted to, but I'd never be able to hide.

When I glanced back to the sidewalk in front of me, Nan had vanished.

So much for my detective skills.

Yet I didn't have to be a detective to know where Nan had gone.

The majestic iron gates of the Paris Cemetery loomed before me. I slipped inside and cut over to Section C, ducking behind the Morris Tomb. From there, I could see Nan sitting beside my grandfather's headstone.

Her lips moved, but I couldn't make out her words. She sipped on her tea and then laughed as if someone had told the funniest story she'd ever heard.

In that moment, I understood what drew Nan to the library every night. It was the perfect cover for a nightly trek to the cemetery.

Memories, Nan had said.

She'd moved in with my parents not long after Grandpa died. Since that time, Nan had told stories about her marriage, including how she and Grandpa would sit and chat after dinner each night, he with his coffee and she with her tea.

Six years after his death, Nan was still sitting with Grandpa after dinner.

For all of her talk about moving on, she hadn't moved an inch.

Nan had grown quiet, and she swiped at her cheeks.

I tiptoed backward, shame washing through me. Even though I hated to see her so sad, this was her time, her space. I had no business watching.

So I walked away, back toward the cab, leaving Nan alone with her memories.

≈

Instead of going back home, I drove toward Bridge Street and pulled Bessie to the side of the road before the ground ended and the river began.

I climbed out of the cab and smoothed the front of my mother's dress. While I typically wouldn't go out for an evening stroll in an outfit more suited to drinks at the country club, there was something to be said for channeling a bit of Audrey Hepburn when you were feeling down.

I skirted the sign proclaiming the bridge closed to pedestrian traffic after dusk and trailed my fingertips along the cool metal railing. The sun had fallen level with the horizon, casting an amber pall across the trees lining the riverbank.

The Delaware glowed as if lit from within, and an eerie mist rose from the water, a clear indication that spring had arrived in Paris.

I reached midspan and stopped, peering between the vertical beams of the weathered suspension bridge like a prisoner, trapped by the uncertainty of my own life.

Nan's question bounced through my brain.

Logic and love suggested I should rush to the nearest airport and book a flight to France, yet I'd done nothing other than leaving a series of voice mail messages.

There *was* the minor detail involving my intense fear of flying. There was also the issue of not knowing where in Paris Fred had gone.

If I channeled my inner Nancy Drew, surely I could figure things out and track the man down, but instead I'd waited... waited for Fred to make the next move.

When had waiting for something to happen become my modus operandi?

Footfalls sounded from a point behind me on the walkway and I tensed.

Ax murderers weren't known for taking after-dinner strolls, were they?

I readied myself, wrapping my fingers around the cab ignition key like a weapon, but when the unknown pedestrian approached, he proved to be something far more unnerving than an attacker.

"Don't mind me." Mick O'Malley's deep voice rumbled through the gathering darkness. "Thought I'd snag a front-row seat in case you decided to swan dive."

"Be still my heart," I said, shooting him a glare.

Mick's tone might have been one of levity, but his features held an expression of worry and deep thought.

"Did you follow me?" I asked.

He moved beside me, leaning on the railing to peer between his own set of vertical bars. "While this town is, in fact, lacking in excitement, I have not yet stooped to stalking you. No."

"I suppose the view out west is a bit more thrilling," I said.

Mick stared straight ahead at the setting sun, the stand of maples and oaks, and the Delaware rushing past. When he turned to meet my stare, our gazes locked for a brief moment. "The view out west has nothing on this."

Unnerved by the intensity in his eyes, I shifted subjects. "How's your mom?"

"Frankie's with her," he answered. "She's some kid."

"My Frankie?" I asked.

Mick nodded, his expression relaxing a measure. "She really has a way with my mom."

"Does she spend time with her often?"

Mick smiled. "All the time. She might surprise you, your little sister."

Oh, she surprised me, all right, even though I was still unable to picture my sister in any mode other than miserable.

We stood in silence for several long moments. I studied the river and then turned to check out the empty bridge behind us.

Not a single car approached the span, but then, that was Paris. A person either lived in Paris, or they didn't. Residents tended to stay for life, and the few who left—like Mick and me—seemed to find their way home sooner or later.

"Why are you here, Mick?" I asked.

"I could ask you the same thing."

"You first."

"I was out for a walk, saw the cab, and wanted to make sure Buddy hadn't decided to end it all at the thought of another Halladay female living under his roof."

I squinted at him. "You always were considerate like that."

A glimmer of mischief danced in his eyes, a brief glimpse into the past. "Your turn," he said.

I shifted my focus to the night sky and hesitated, fighting the urge to tell him everything, just like old times. I reminded myself that I hadn't seen the man in a dozen years, even though standing beside him made me feel as though no time had passed at all.

"Nan asked me a question, and I came up here to think about my answer."

"And?" Mick asked.

"I'm still thinking."

He said nothing, but the look of anticipation he wore told me he knew I'd crack.

"Don't you have anyone else down on her luck you could interrogate?" I asked.

Mick's rich laughter echoed through the night sky. "I'm all yours tonight, Halladay," he said.

A shiver raced across my shoulders, and I suspected it had nothing to do with my lack of jacket and everything to do with Mick's words.

Mick shrugged out of his denim jacket and draped it across my shoulders, the move so familiar, so natural, it made me ache.

He shoved his hands in his pockets and dropped his voice low. "Start sharing, Halladay. We're burning nighttime."

I took a deep breath and began. "Well, you already know about Fred."

I looked to Mick for a response and he nodded. Good enough.

"And I lost my column because obviously I'm not hip enough to pull in buckets of readers."

Another look. This time a shrug.

"Then there's the issue of the house." I threw my hands up in the air. "Apparently the termites caused so much damage it's not safe for me to move in."

"Feel better?" he asked.

"Starting to," I said; then I continued. "Tonight, my mother invited Ted Miller to dinner. Want to know why?"

He nodded. Good man.

"Because he's an eligible bachelor, and she's not about to let the deposit on the country club go to waste."

At this, Mick spoke. "So she doesn't have a lot of faith in your fiancé?"

I shook my head. "Apparently not."

Mick's dark brows lifted toward his hairline. "Tough break, Halladay."

"Then I saw Nan sitting all alone by Grandpa's grave." Sudden tears welled in my eyes. "That just makes me sad."

Mick frowned, obviously taken aback by my sudden water-works. "Hey, hey." He reached for me, but pulled back without making contact. "You'll figure it all out, Abby."

I'd heard that before.

I shook my head and gathered myself, not wanting to add "full meltdown" to my list of accomplishments.

"I should take the cab back," I said. "You want a lift?"

Mick shook his head. "Nice night for a walk."

Our eyes met and held.

For a moment, I felt transported back to high school, back to the countless heartfelt conversations Mick and I had shared. There had been a time when we'd told each other every hope, dream, or plan that had crossed our minds.

Then thirteen years had passed in silence.

"Thanks for listening," I said, even as regret and sadness simmered to life inside me.

Mick gave me a dismissive shrug before he turned to leave.

"Your jacket," I called out as his long stride quickly length-ened the space between us.

"You keep it," he answered without turning around. "Looks like it belongs on you."

Before my brain could formulate so much as a thank-you, he was gone—vanished into the mist swirling in from the river.

I stood still, letting my emotions settle inside me. Then I slipped my arms into the sleeves of his well-worn jacket, breathed in Mick's scent, and headed for home.

CHAPTER NINE

—— —— ——

I accomplished two things over the weekend.

I'd picked up my car from the municipal lot and parked it over in the yellow Victorian's gravel drive. Structural damage might keep me out of the house for a bit longer, but at least the car could sit in its new driveway. Plus, I'd begun to enjoy driving the cab, not that I was ready to admit that to anyone.

Second, I'd spent the weekend plotting the rebuilding of my life.

Destiny's blunt but accurate words bounced through my brain as I broke down exactly what I needed to do. I needed to get the house fixed. I needed to pitch a new column to Max Campbell. I needed to make a decision about Fred.

I was not about to jump on a plane to France, so I left him a series of messages in which I shared my plans and explained the fact that my new, nonboring life would be ready to share with him when he was ready to return.

On Monday afternoon, Mom knocked on the edge of my bedroom door. "Abby, go get Frankie, please," she said, standing just inside my room. "Mrs. Pierce will be here any minute."

Isabel Pierce had been giving piano lessons since the Paris forefathers had been tying their horses next to the Paris Inn.

While that might have been a slight exaggeration, it wasn't much of one. And Madeline Halladay believed a cultured woman was one able to perform a piano concerto at the drop of a hat. I'd sat through years of Mrs. Pierce's lessons, and, as much as I'd never admit it, I was glad I knew how to play.

Frankie, however, sat through her piano lessons with Mrs. Pierce and then raced back to her secondhand guitar as quickly as she could.

"She's probably over with Mrs. O'Malley," Mom said. "Tell her she has five minutes."

"Why does she spend so much time with Mick's mom?"

Mom's eyes turned soft. "They have a special bond." She smiled. "Mrs. O'Malley loves your sister for exactly who she is."

Mom walked away, but I hesitated momentarily, wondering if her words had been meant for me. Did I even know who my younger sister was these days?

I slid off my bed and headed downstairs.

Dad had left his favorite red-white-and-blue plaid fedora on the credenza in the hall beside the cab keys, and I grabbed it. I shoved the hat on my head, hoping to disguise the fact I hadn't brushed my messy hair that morning.

I covered the ground between houses as I always had—by cutting through the gap in the O'Malleys' hedge. I headed for the back door to their kitchen, remembering how pots of bright impatiens and daisies once framed the brilliant cobalt-blue door.

The pots sat empty, save for what remained of the forgotten soil, now spotted with patches of green moss.

When no one answered my knock, I pushed inside as I'd done so many times before.

I leaned into the kitchen, the smell of burned coffee pungent in the air. "Hello?" I called out. "Mrs. O'Malley? Frankie?"

Nothing.

I tried again, stepping inside and pushing the door shut behind me. "Mick? Mrs. O'Malley?"

A lone picture hung on the face of a battered Frigidaire, anchored by a smiley-face magnet, and I moved closer. In the snapshot, a preteen Mick, his mother, and father stood beneath the old maple outside, their forced smiles belying their linked arms.

Stop snooping, I thought to myself. I headed for the center hall and called out again, "Frankie? Time to head home."

Nothing.

Nothing but the soft sound of music, coming from the slightly ajar door to the basement.

I followed the sound, hesitating at the top step.

Even though I'd spent much of my youth inside this house traipsing up and down these basement steps for tree house supplies, I was no longer a child, and Mick was no longer my favorite diversion.

I pulled the door open a bit wider and peered down the old wooden steps. Strains of Little Feat came from below.

I was fairly certain the music selection had little to do with Mrs. O'Malley and everything to do with Mick.

I took a step nonetheless. "Frankie?"

The wooden steps creaked beneath my clogs as I descended, my focus zeroing in on the old Formica table sitting against the far wall. I cleared the bottom step and hesitated, taking in the sight of the smooth, marbled top, illuminated only by a single bare bulb dangling from the beamed ceiling above.

I remembered when this particular piece of furniture held a place of prominence upstairs in the O'Malley kitchen. Mick and I had spent hours at this table crafting No Adults Allowed signs for the tree house.

I ran my fingertips across the surface, remembering how we'd built our first science project together there—a working volcano that erupted two blocks from school when the ingredients shifted.

I'd sat at this table with my parents and Mrs. O'Malley the night Mick's father died, feeling helpless to erase the pain and heartache in her eyes.

Mick was long gone by the time his father wrecked his car. He hadn't said good-bye. He hadn't written, called, or said a word to me during the time he'd been gone.

And he hadn't come home to pay his final respects to his father.

My gaze landed on the items spread across the tabletop.

Pliers. Safety glasses. Cut glass. Soldering tools.

I frowned, reaching for a glistening triangle of green glass.

"I thought you learned your lesson about breaking and entering."

Mick's voice sounded from the stairs behind me, and my heart fell to my toes. The triangle slipped from my grip, hitting the tabletop with a dull *crack*.

I picked up the piece, the flawless glass now marred by a hairline fracture. I spun to face Mick, heat firing in my cheeks. "I was looking for Frankie."

His dark eyes narrowed, full of disbelief. "In the basement?"

I winced. "I heard the music."

"Big Little Feat fan, is she?"

I shrugged, realizing he wasn't going to let me get away easily. "I might have been…"

"Snooping?"

I shook my head. "I wouldn't call it snooping."

We stared at each other for several long, uncomfortable seconds before Mick turned to make room for me on the steps. "They're out back in the greenhouse." He pointed up toward the kitchen.

I gestured to the spread of materials on the table. "Are these yours?"

He shifted his focus to the work area. "My mother's."

"Oh." I glanced back at the tools and supplies, imagining how Mrs. O'Malley might have once loved making her own stained-glass creations. "She must miss this."

Mick's expression turned heartbreakingly sad. "You can't miss what you don't remember."

"I'm so sorry." I took a step toward him, but he shuttered his features, firmly sliding his protective wall back into place.

"Be sure to shut the kitchen door behind you. Wouldn't want people wandering in off the street."

I handed Mick the cracked triangle. He studied it momentarily before fisting his hand around the damaged piece.

"I'm sorry," I said. "I wish I could fix it."

He stared at me, resignation in his eyes. "You can't fix everything."

"Well, I'm sorry," I said again, as I pushed past him and headed up the steps.

"Nice hat, Halladay," he said.

I supposed that was the same as good-bye.

I tried not to let the door hit me on the ass as I fled the O'Malleys' kitchen. True to Mick's word, I found Frankie and his mother sitting side by side inside the battered greenhouse.

They hadn't seen me yet, so I stood just outside the door, listening. The only sound from inside was the music of Frankie's guitar, her softly strummed notes lifting from the depths of the space filled completely with dead plants.

Perhaps they were the botanical ghosts of flowers and shrubs gone by, or perhaps Detta O'Malley had been doing a whole lot more trash-picking than I'd imagined, but the greenhouse was packed.

Someone sang softly, and I recognized Mrs. O'Malley's voice instantly, her heartfelt words bringing back the rush of joy I'd witnessed when she'd sung in Dad's cab.

To my utter surprise, Frankie joined in, harmonizing beautifully as the two sang a Beatles tune Mrs. O'Malley used to sing as she worked in her garden.

"There are places I remember…"

The scene before me amazed me, and my brain barely knew where to begin to process the pieces.

The music rang out in direct opposition to the expanse of dead and decaying plants. I had never heard my sister sing anything, let alone a lovely ballad.

"…I love you more."

Frankie looked into Detta's face and smiled, her joy palpable in her features and her body's swaying to the music.

Mick's words on the bridge echoed through my mind. *She's some kid.*

She was, and I'd had no idea.

"Will you look at that?"

My mother's voice sounded softly from behind me, startling me with her nearness.

"I didn't hear you sneak up," I whispered.

"Years of practice." She grinned, tipping her chin toward Frankie. "When's the last time you saw your sister this happy?"

"I know." I nodded, loving the genuine emotion of the moment. "It's been a long time."

While my mother and I might not have been able to make out all the notes or words, we had no trouble understanding the impact of the music.

Both Frankie and Mrs. O'Malley beamed, their voices lifting together above the collection of dead plants.

In that moment, I saw a mature, confident, happy side of my sister I'd never seen before. Pride welled up inside me.

As for Mrs. O'Malley, she glowed as if lit from within, transformed by the music just as she'd been that day in Dad's cab.

"I need to write this down," Mom whispered.

I frowned. "What do you mean?"

"In my journal." She tapped on my shoulder and gestured for me to follow her outside.

"What journal?" I asked, once we were out of earshot.

"My gratitude journal." She shrugged. "You should try it. Come on," she said, stepping out toward our house. "Let's give them a little privacy."

"What about Mrs. Pierce?" I asked, stunned by mother's newly rebellious attitude.

My mom simply laughed softly and reached for my hand. "Mrs. Pierce can wait."

❧

That night, I thought about Mom's gratitude journal.

I thought about my parents and how readily they'd welcomed me home. I thought about Mick and how carelessly I'd handled his mother's supplies. I thought about Frankie and how wrong I'd been in my assessment of my own sister.

When I called Fred, I left a message a bit less about my plans and a bit more about life. I told him about what I'd seen inside Mrs. O'Malley's greenhouse. I described the setting and the beauty of the song. In my one-sided conversation, I relived the moment, and how proud I was of my little sister.

And then I left Fred with a parting thought.

"Seeing them like that got me to thinking," I said. "Maybe you're not bored because of a lack of life. Maybe you're bored because of a lack of appreciation."

I hesitated for a beat, then finished the call. "Anyway, I hope you're doing all right."

I disconnected, and as I put away my phone, I realized that I had a thing or two to learn about appreciation myself.

CHAPTER TEN

___ ___ ___

I found myself at Max Campbell's office the next morning, asking for my job back.

It had only been six days since I'd listened to Max tell me my column was finished. As I took in my surroundings, it felt as though it had been years.

A lot had happened in the past week.

As I made my case for kindness and decorum in today's society, Nan's question still remained lodged in my brain.

What are you going to do now?

Darn the woman.

So here I paced, attempting to start my rebuilding process.

Max, unfortunately, had other ideas.

"I'm sorry, Abby," he said. "The readers in our market want grit. They want more than some Pollyanna encouraging them to only speak kind thoughts. Let's face it, edgy you're not." He waved one hand dismissively. "No offense."

"None taken," I answered, even as I realized I'd been called boring and labeled a Pollyanna, all in one sentence. "I can do edgy," I insisted, hating the way my voice cracked on the word *edgy.*

I'd shoved Dad's fedora into my bag and pulled it out now, tugging it down over my hair. "See? I can do edgy."

Max's lips quirked, but he had the decency to remain otherwise expressionless. "A plaid fedora does not make you edgy."

But I wasn't about to be dismissed so easily. I narrowed my eyes and forged ahead. "This hat is just the beginning of the new me…the edgy me. Let me tell you about my life since we last met."

His eyebrows arched.

"Fred ran off to Europe. I've been chased out of our new house by termite-induced structural damage." I paced faster, the words pouring out of me. "I've taken to driving my father's cab simply because I like the monster car, and my mother has already invited one of the town's bachelors to dinner."

I spun on one heel to face him, planting my palms on the edge of his desk and leaning—dare I say it—edgily toward his amused expression.

"I can do edgy," I repeated.

Max sat back, probably wanting to put as much space between us as possible. Then he spoke. "Come back to me with some fresh ideas, Abby, and we'll talk. But your old column is finished."

I shook his hand and assured him I could deliver exactly what he needed, even as I wondered what in the world that might be. One minute I was selling decorum and the next minute I'd sold out for edgy.

I passed Rosie Henderson, Living Section, on my way to the elevator. She took one look at my fedora and frowned. "Bad hair day?"

Bite me, I thought. But instead, I said, "Have a nice day, Rosie."

"Not edgy," Max called out from his office as I walked away.

I spent the day running short hops between the Trenton train station and nearby towns. I also stopped by the borough clerk's office to fill out my taxi license application and be fingerprinted. In a town like Paris, the process was more of a formality than anything else, but if I was going to drive Dad's cab, I was going to do it right.

I noticed movement in the tree house as I pulled into my parents' drive. I parked the Beast and headed out front, surprised to find Mick, feet dangling over the side, working on a large spiral-bound pad of some sort.

"What are you doing?" I yelled up.

"Hiding from you," he answered.

I smiled, glad to hear his return to banter. "How's that working out for you?"

"So far, not so good." He laughed, shut the notebook, and tucked it behind his back.

"What's in the notebook?" I pointed.

Mick grinned and shook his head. Then he climbed down the ladder with ease and coordination, two things I had never mastered. "Not everything's your business, Halladay. Tough day on the roads?"

I thought about how peaceful the return drive to Paris had been. At some point during the past several years, I'd stopped appreciating the beauty of the area. Just today, I'd passed an alpaca pasture, an arboretum, and rolling valleys that quite simply had stolen my breath.

Truth be told, I was enjoying driving Dad's cab far more than I ever imagined possible.

"It's not so bad. You meet a lot of interesting people."

"And they, in turn, meet you"—Mick pointed at my hat—"and your hat."

"It's the official cabbie hat for Halladay Cabs," I said, bluffing on the fly. "How's your mom?"

"She's out back with your sister." He turned and headed for his house.

"I was wrong about snooping in your basement," I called after him. "I'm sorry."

Mick came to a stop and turned to face me. His smile faded. "Let it go, Abby. It's over."

"I still feel bad about the glass."

Mick's throat worked, and I suspected his thoughts had gone to the other damaged areas of his life. A shadow passed across his features. "Things break." He forced a smile. "That's life." He turned away again. "I have to start dinner. See you later, Abby."

Suddenly, I thought of part two of my rebuilding plan, an area in which I definitely needed help.

"Hey, Mick," I called out.

This time he stopped without turning.

"Do you think you could help me handle the damage to my house?"

No response.

"Please?" I added.

His face tipped toward the sky, and even though his back was toward me, I could picture the expression on his features.

"Well?" I asked, closing the gap between us.

He turned to face me, his eyebrows furrowed, as if he were debating the issue in his head.

"I'll never be able to fix my life if I can't fix my house," I said. He'd once told me I had a way of wearing people down. With any luck, I hadn't lost my touch.

Mick chuckled softly. "You always loved the drama." Then he hesitated before he spoke again. "Whose life, Abby? Yours? Or the one you'd planned with your fiancé?"

The moment of truth. What did they call that in the movies? A turning point?

This moment felt like mine.

"My life," I said softly, so softly I could barely hear my own words.

I'd set about fixing my life with the vision of Fred's return front and center in my mind, yet as I'd started to move forward, Fred's image had started to fade.

My pulse quickened and I pulled myself up taller.

I was fixing my life for *me*.

Mick patted me on the head, bringing back a rush of emotion and memories so thick I felt my knees go weak.

"Meet me at your house at eight o'clock Thursday morning."

"Okay." I nodded.

Then he grinned. "*Your* house. Not your parents' house."

"Got it."

"We're going to assess the damage and do a walk-through with a contractor. You'll get your house fixed."

"Thanks, Mick." I turned to leave before he saw just how deeply our interaction had affected me.

"Abby."

His voice stopped me in my tracks.

"I'll help you fix your house," he said. "Fixing your life is all yours."

CHAPTER ELEVEN

— — —

Instead of breakfast with my family the next morning, I headed for Jessica's café.

The morning crowd was thick, and my friend worked the room expertly, serving up eggs, laughter, and hospitality like no one else could.

She spotted me the instant I cleared the threshold, and my large coffee sat waiting on the breakfast bar by the time I crossed the room.

"Fred?" she asked, soft lines of concern framing her blue eyes.

"Silent," I answered.

"Work?" she asked.

"Max said he'll look at some ideas."

She patted my hand encouragingly. "Termites?"

"Dead." I frowned. "The damage is major. Mick's helping me meet with a contractor tomorrow." I waved my hand dismissively. "Enough about me. Tell me what's going on in your world."

Her sigh took me by surprise. "Things have been a little slow, actually. I'm getting worried."

"Slow?" I looked around the restaurant. Every booth and table but three was busy. "The joint is jumping."

"Business is down 13.8 percent from this time last year."

I took a long swallow of coffee. "I think you're doing great."

She jerked a thumb toward the new restaurant across the street. We stared through the front window, taking in the view over at Johnny's Test Kitchen. Johnny Testa, a New York hotshot, had left the bustle of the big city behind to settle in Paris, choosing the corner opposite the Paris Café for his newest venture.

A steady stream of traffic flowed in and out of the competition's cherry-red front door.

"What can he possibly be doing better than you?" I asked.

"Fast food," Jessica answered. "Good food."

"Isn't that exactly what you serve?"

She shook her head and her blond ponytail swished from side to side. "I serve good food slow. I encourage my customers to come and sit for a while. To visit. To relax. To make the Paris Café their home away from home."

She'd rebuilt her life here, and in so doing, she'd created a place like no other.

As far as I could tell, her business was as steady as it had ever been, no matter what her numbers said. I couldn't help but wonder whether she felt threatened by the restaurant competition or by the restaurateur—a man who no doubt brought back memories of her ex-husband.

"I'd pick eating here over fast food any day," I said.

"Good food fast," she corrected me. "I'd better get back to work."

"Jessica?"

Her eyebrows lifted, waiting for the rest of my question.

"When did you feel happy again?"

She smiled and blew out a sigh, knowing instantly exactly what I was asking.

She reached out to take my hand. "When I learned to love the life I had instead of the life I'd lost."

That night, Madeline Halladay's parade of unsuitable bachelors continued. In a town as small as Paris, however, even my mother was bound to come up short on available candidates.

"A little off the sides and you'll be a new woman." Manny the barber waved his fork at my hair as he spoke. Then he shoveled another forkful into his mouth. "This is delicious," he said. "What do you call this?"

"Meat loaf," my mother answered, and I couldn't help but notice that even she had been left borderline speechless by the speed with which the man put away his food.

Manny had taken over the local barbershop a few years earlier. He and I had met a few times at karaoke night, but other than that, we hadn't had much occasion to become acquainted. From what I understood, he'd won over the town with his easy chatter, dedication to hair, and reasonable prices.

I wondered how many Paris residents had ever seen Manny eat.

"Delicious," he said, sending a spray of food across the table in my direction.

Frankie seized the opportunity to excuse herself. My father, mesmerized by Manny's mastication, said nothing to stop her.

A hand locked on my knee beneath the table and squeezed. I met my mother's apologetic glance and relaxed a bit. Even she knew tonight's guest wouldn't be kneeling beside me at the altar anytime soon.

"So I hear good old Fred left you high and dry," Manny said.

So much for feeling relaxed.

"He'll be back," I answered, but I believed the words less and less with every day that passed.

"Pack your puppets, you're going to Paris," Missy said, doing her best television game show host voice.

"Puppets?" Manny asked.

My mother shook her head and took a swallow of her wine. "She's been watching too much Game Show Network."

Manny laughed, a hearty, bellowing sound that shook the chandelier above our heads. "No such thing as too much Game Show Network."

Then Manny shifted gears entirely.

"What about your column?" he asked. "I used to think you could use a little more oomph in your responses, but I do miss seeing your name in the paper. When are they bringing it back?"

"You read my column?" I brightened a bit before I answered Manny's question. At least I'd had one confirmed reader. "I met with my managing editor, Max, yesterday," I continued. "Basically, unless I can present him with new ideas that will bring in readers, I should start dusting off my résumé."

"Then dust away, doll," Manny said, erasing my affection for him as a reader. His features grew serious. "How are you at cutting hair?"

I shook my head. "Not good."

"So what's the plan?" Manny asked. "No job. No guy. Living at home. Seems to me you've got some work to do."

No kidding I had work to do, but I really didn't need Manny to tell me that.

I turned my focus to my dad instead. "I think I'd like to keep driving mornings, if that's all right."

Dad nodded and shot me a wink.

Manny let loose with another belly laugh. "Cabby Abby." He slapped the table and his spoon flipped to the carpet. "That's perfect."

Manny made no move to retrieve his spoon, so my mother subtly plucked the utensil from the floor on her way to the kitchen. "I've got strawberry shortcake for dessert. Can I bring everyone a dish?"

Manny patted his belly and shook his head. "Oh, I couldn't. I'm full from dinner." My pulse quickened at the thought that my inquisition might soon be over, but then he tipped his well-coiffed head to one side and shot me a wink. "On second thought, how about a small piece? That'll give us more time to visit. Right, Cabby Abby?"

"Right," I said, raising my water glass with faux cheer. "Can't wait."

CHAPTER TWELVE

For the first time since I'd turned eight, my mother excused me from helping with the dishes. Apparently, Manny's words rang just as loudly in her ears as they did in mine.

So what's the plan? No job. No guy. Living at home. Seems to me you've got some work to do.

After dinner with Manny, I needed to get out. I needed to be anywhere but inside my parents' house, faced with the reality the local barber had a better grasp on the implosion that was my life than I did.

I thought about doing a pop-in at Jessica's apartment, but she was probably in the midst of getting Max and Bella ready for bed. The last thing she needed was an unexpected guest.

Even though we didn't typically hang out without Jessica, I called Destiny and headed for the Pub.

"So how are things going?" I asked as we sat down, always nervous at the first few moments of conversation with Destiny.

"Things?" she asked.

And that was why. The woman was incapable of giving a straight answer.

"At work," I answered. "With your customers."

She pursed her lips. "A bit slow, actually."

"Seems to be a lot of that going around."

Destiny said nothing, merely squinted at me, as if she were waiting for the show to begin.

I waited until she took a drink before I asked my next question.

"Am I boring?"

Destiny choked on her beer.

"I thought we were here for a fun night out, not a round of *This Is Your Life*."

She'd lost her usual ball cap for the evening, twisting her mahogany hair into a knot at the nape of her neck that made her look far more stunning than I was used to. If I hadn't known Destiny most of my life, I might have found her intimidating. Heck, I have known her most of my life, and I *do* find her intimidating.

"I think I used to be more fun," I said.

She nodded. "Your point?"

I narrowed my eyes at her. "Were you always this obtuse?"

She grinned and took another swallow of beer, straight from the bottle. "Were you?"

I studied her, taking my time before I answered. Her dark gaze waited for me to find my own answer, even though, in my heart of hearts, I'd already found it.

I'd found my answer every time I left another message for Fred. I'd found my answer watching Frankie and Mrs. O'Malley living in the moment.

The answer was that I used to know how to live.

I used to get up onstage for karaoke night. I used to sing more, laugh more, and live more. I used to plan less.

Hell, I'd done jail time.

The harsh reality settled in the pit of my stomach. Somewhere along the way, I'd become the person I thought I should be.

"I want me back," I said.

Destiny leaned over, slapped my shoulder, and snatched my wineglass.

She put her fingers to her lips and whistled. Every head in the Pub turned, but Destiny paid no mind. I loved that about her.

"Jerry," she called out, "would you please bring my friend a beer?"

Jerry winked from where he worked at the end of the bar, then slid a bottle of Corona in my direction. I snagged it, took a long drink, and savored the feel of the familiar, cold beverage gliding down my throat.

"Corona is good," I said, pressing a kiss to the side of the cold bottle.

"Welcome back," Destiny said. "What's your next move?"

I told her about my visit to the *Times* and my mother's two dinner guests. I told her about my calls to Fred and about how much I'd enjoyed driving Dad's cab.

Much to her credit, Destiny sat quietly as she listened to me unload the events of the past week. After I finished, I waited for her to hand down her advice, but she said nothing.

"Aren't you going to tell me what to do?" I asked.

"Been there, done that."

She'd no sooner spoken than Jerry announced the start of karaoke night. I found it difficult to believe I'd sat in this very spot one week earlier, shell-shocked by the events of that day.

Since then, I'd had time to process a little of what had happened. I'd had time to listen, to watch, to learn.

Maybe the time had come to dive back in, Fred or no Fred.

Pat Benatar's "Heartbreaker" blared out through the sound system, and I started to sing along, softly at first, then more loudly, enjoying the moment.

"Go for it." Destiny tipped her beer toward the stage.

"Want to come with me?" I asked.

She shook her head. "Not on my bucket list."

I'd missed the sign-up but knew that didn't matter. When I raised my hand to snag Jerry's attention, I kicked at Destiny's stool. "Come on."

"Special guest, Abigail Halladay," Jerry called out, having grabbed the microphone to perform the double duty he pulled every karaoke night. "You're next."

I reached for Destiny's arm, but she pushed me away. "Go be you."

An odd sensation fluttered deep in my belly, and I hesitated. I'd watched from the sidelines for so long, I wasn't sure I could remember how to be onstage.

Destiny leaned close. "There's a difference between maturity and living like a corpse."

She was right.

I hopped down from my stool and headed for the small stage, pausing long enough to give Jerry my song choice.

Applause filled the air, pushing me forward. I stepped up on the wooden platform, grabbed the microphone, blinked against the glare of the lone spotlight, and waved to the crowd.

For one fleeting second, I felt victorious. I felt free. I felt alive.

Then I began to count faces, couples, clusters of Paris residents, all staring at *me*.

What were they thinking? That I was a failure? That I was bound to screw this up just like I'd screwed up my engagement, my career, and my choice of home?

I wasn't sure whether my brain shut off before I stopped breathing or after, but all I could envision in that moment was the smirk on Max Campbell's face when I'd called myself edgy.

All I could hear in my mind was Fred's voice, crackling across the overseas connection, telling me how bored he was.

He was right. Max was right. I wasn't edgy. I was boring.

I'd been crazy to climb up onstage.

Words scrolled across the video screen as the speakers blared Helen Reddy's "I Am Woman." Yet, there I stood. Doing nothing.

"Abigail Halladay," Jerry called out again, probably hoping he could shock me into action.

He hoped wrong.

I held my ground, the microphone white-knuckled in my grip, and I did nothing. I said nothing. I sang nothing.

Jerry had the decency to lower the volume until the song faded away. The audience, all of whom had sat in uncomfortable silence watching me freeze, clapped politely as I hooked the microphone back on its stand and stepped off the stage.

As I reached my place at the bar, Destiny handed me my beer and tipped her head to one side. "Guess you won't need the make-an-ass-of-yourself-in-public coupon I've been saving for you."

"Thanks for your support," I said, climbing back up on the stool.

I sat, shoulders slumped, watching from the sidelines as the rest of karaoke night went on without me.

CHAPTER THIRTEEN

—— —— ——

When I woke the next morning, I rolled over and looked at the clock. Seven fifteen. I had forty-five minutes to shower, dress, and meet Mick at my termite-ravaged house.

A short while later, I stuffed one of my mother's chocolate-chip muffins in my mouth and headed for the cab keys.

My father's fedora sat neatly on the corner of the credenza, the Beast's keys tucked just beneath the brim.

The fedora, much like Bessie, had been officially off-limits for as long as I could remember. But now, Dad had entrusted me with not one, but two of his most prized possessions.

Had I even said thank you?

"Mom?" I called out. "Where's Dad?"

I heard Madeline O'Malley's muffled answer from the mud-room, but I had zero idea of what she'd said. When I rounded the corner, I could barely believe my eyes.

My mother's cheeks appeared stuffed, and muffin crumbs marred her perfect lipstick. Even more astonishingly, her apron appeared wrinkled. Rumpled, even.

"Mom?" I said cautiously. "Are you all right?"

She nodded, but in her eyes I spotted the faintest trace of tears. I crossed to where she stood and wrapped her in a bear hug, something I'd done routinely in my youth, but hadn't done in…well…I honestly couldn't remember how long.

"What's wrong?" I asked.

But my mother had slapped her mask of perfection back into place. "Just doing some quality assurance, honey." She hugged me back, straightened, brushed the crumbs from her mouth, and smiled. "In answer to your question, your father went out for another ride."

"To where?" I pushed.

She forced a smile. "Your guess is as good as mine, darling."

"Did you ask him?"

She shrugged. "He's exercising. It's a good thing."

Our gazes locked and held. My mother might talk a good game, but there was no way the man was taking four- and five-hour rides.

"Where are you headed today, honey?" she asked, ever the queen of diversion.

"I'm meeting a contractor over at my house."

"Have a nice day," she called out as I headed for the hall.

She could pretend to be June Cleaver all she wanted, but sooner or later, she was bound to crack.

A few minutes later, I climbed out of the Beast and headed up the center walk toward my house. An unfamiliar pickup truck sat parked in the gravel driveway.

I followed the sound of voices around to the back of the house, where Mick stood deep in conversation with Chuck Matthews, a local contractor.

"There she is now," Mick said. He leaned close as I stepped up to shake Chuck's hand. "Nice hat, Halladay."

I shot him a glare, but he'd already looked past me, pointing to where the back wall of the house met the foundation. "Let's get started."

Chuck tapped the wall with the toe of his work boot and nodded in my direction. "Frank was right; there's a definite problem with the sill. You'd better come here."

Mick squatted down, and I matched his move. Chuck pointed out the weakened areas of board that topped the foundation, detailing how each would have to be reinforced or replaced.

My stomach sank. If the foundation held up the house and the damaged board sat between the foundation and walls, surely this couldn't be good.

"How bad is this?" I asked.

Mick reached over and squeezed my knee, the move taking me by complete surprise. "Not good," he said under his breath as he pushed to standing.

"I pulled some boards in the basement this morning. Chuck took a look before you got here." His focus zeroed in on the contractor. "Trouble in the joists? Or do you think our troubles are mainly here?"

Mainly here? Wasn't here bad enough? I mean, we were looking at a damaged piece of wood that appeared to bear the load of the entire house.

I wasn't a builder—or an architect—but I suddenly found myself filled with the realization that I might be living under the Halladay roof a lot longer than I'd anticipated.

"You've definitely got trouble," Chuck said, heading for the basement entrance. "I'll show you."

He disappeared down the steps and Mick moved to follow, but then he stopped, apparently realizing I hadn't moved a muscle.

If the basic support structure of the house was damaged, what was to prevent the entire thing from collapsing?

Jessica had been right about moving to Paris. I'd pushed Fred to agree that the small Victorian was a good investment. But this... How would I ever tell him about this?

I swallowed, a quick wave of queasiness washing through me.

"Come on." Mick held out his hand. "You can fix this. Remember?"

I met his gaze and saw the kind patience I'd clung to all those years ago, each time he tried to teach me to play baseball, or master the rope swing, or go tubing on the river.

But then I saw something else.

I saw Mick, the man.

He was no longer the boy I'd followed around like a puppy dog. He was a man who had built a life for himself on the opposite coast, even if that life hadn't played out the way he'd hoped.

He was a man who had come home to take care of his mother, and now stood at the entrance to termite hell, doing his best to help me.

I snapped myself from my trance and nodded, even though I wanted nothing more than to run the other way and leave Mick to fix this without me.

I followed him into the basement, staring numbly, watching as Chuck spot-checked boards that revealed an area of subfloor and support joists that looked more like lace than they did lumber capable of supporting a house.

"Abby?"

Mick's voice pulled me from the downward spiral of my thoughts, and I blew out a breath.

"What's your thought on time line? I was just telling Chuck that I'm only here for moral support. This house belongs to you. Well…you and Fred."

The three of us knew I was in completely over my head. Literally. Yet there Mick stood, trying to infuse me with a sense of authority and competency I didn't feel.

"What do you think, Chuck?" I asked. "What have you found with other cases like this one?"

Chuck snapped his tongue and shook his head. "Never seen one this bad, but I'm thinking we can replace these joists and the flooring above in two weeks. Maybe a month if the first-floor walls are involved."

I chose to ignore the fact the house held the worst termite damage he'd seen and focused on the positive. He could fix this.

"Okay, then. I'd like to see an estimate and your plans by Monday." I turned to leave, wanting to be safely inside the Beast before the sheer horror of seeing the destroyed beams and boards hit me. "I've got a cab to drive."

I waved over my shoulder. "Mick, thanks for your help today. Chuck, I'll speak to you Monday."

I waited until I'd driven down the street and onto Stone Lane. Then I pulled the cab to the side of road, cut the ignition, and cried.

CHAPTER FOURTEEN

— — —

Later that afternoon, the gray skies opened and a heavy spring rain inundated Paris.

The Beast and I had run a fare down to the Trenton train station and were taking a shortcut back to Jessica's for a quick cup of coffee when the atmosphere crackled with thunder.

A medium-size border collie raced to the curb, perilously close to the street. I braked hard, but the dog sat, apparently never intending to dash into traffic. He raised a paw and tipped his lovely head to one side, as if he wanted me to stop.

A gray-haired gentleman stepped to the curb behind the dog. He held a folded newspaper over his head and smiled even though the skies had opened and the deluge had begun.

I leaned across the massive bench seat, cranked down the window, and shouted, "Do you need a lift?"

"Afraid I left my wallet at home," he answered.

I glanced from the man to his soaking-wet dog and back again. Dad would kill me if I got wet-dog smell inside the Beast. But he also had a firm policy about helping those in need. This man and his dog were definitely in need.

"On the house," I called out, gesturing for the pair to climb inside.

The dog bounded across the backseat the instant the door opened.

"Apologies for getting this beautiful automobile wet," the gentleman said.

I turned to face him and smiled. "No worries. I'm just glad I came along when I did. This isn't my usual route."

"Must be our lucky day." He gave the dog a quick pet. "Eh, Riley?"

Riley rested his chin on the back of my seat, and I stroked his nose. "He's beautiful." I shifted my attention to my human passenger. "Where can I take you?"

"We're headed to the Widow Murphy's. Are you familiar with that address?"

I nodded. "That I am."

I pulled away from the curb and thought about a time when the Widow Murphy had been the go-to resource for anything a person wanted to know about Paris—from town politics to interfamilial feuds.

Sadly, time had not been kind to the widow's health. She'd once run the town museum that sat next to the library, but she now spent most days sitting on her front porch, watching traffic slide past.

I heard my passenger struggle with the drenched newspaper in his lap. "I'm afraid we won't be doing her puzzles today," he said.

"Might I ask how you know Mrs. Murphy?"

"Absolutely," the man answered, reaching out to pet his dog. "Riley and I are a team. He's a therapy dog, and Mrs. Murphy has become one of his favorite stops."

"Therapy dog?"

The gentleman nodded. "He's a great listener."

I glanced up into the rearview mirror as I drove, catching his nod. The skin around the older man's eyes crinkled. "Everyone likes to be listened to."

I thought of Frankie and Mrs. O'Malley. I thought of the messages I left Fred every night. I thought of how Mick had let me call the shots that morning.

My passenger was absolutely correct.

"I'm Abby Halladay," I said. "Nice to meet you."

"Don Michaels," he answered. "I'm renting a place out on Creek Road until I can find a place of my own."

"How long have you been in town?"

"A few months now," he answered.

"What brings you to Paris?"

"My wife and I always loved to visit." He fell silent for a moment. "She's been gone four years."

I thought of Nan and her nightly visits to the cemetery and wondered if Don Michaels suffered from a similar grief. "I'm sorry."

I slowed the Beast for a stop sign, stealing another glance at the mirror.

Mr. Michaels pulled a handkerchief from his pocket and meticulously wiped down the Beast's leather seat. "The heart never forgets," he said. "But in time it makes room to live again." He folded his handkerchief into a neat square and smiled up at me in the rearview mirror.

"Well, welcome to Paris," I said as I refocused on my driving.

We traveled in comfortable silence as I maneuvered the Beast through the storm toward the outskirts of town near the river. As kids, we used to joke that the Widow Murphy fancied herself the guard of Paris, living on the literal edge of town.

"Fate's a funny thing, isn't it?" Don asked.

I gave a slight shrug. Fate hadn't given me much to laugh about lately.

"If you hadn't taken a different route today," he continued, "Riley and I would never have made your acquaintance."

He was right. I smiled at the simple wisdom of his statement.

"Here we are," I said, as we pulled in front of the widow's redbrick colonial. The trees lining the riverbank swayed in the storm's wind gusts, and the rushing river roared above the noise of the downpour.

Don Michaels opened the door to leave.

"I apologize for my inability to pay you." He frowned.

"Your company was my payment." I extended my hand. "It's been my pleasure to meet you."

"The pleasure was all mine, Abby Halladay." He took my hand and gave it a solid shake. "May our paths cross again someday."

"I'd like that."

I watched Don and Riley climb out into the storm.

I waited until they crossed the wide, wet front yard, and then I drove away.

That night, after Nan returned from the library, I found her sitting on the floor of her bedroom, sorting through the contents of a hatbox.

I stood in the doorway for a moment, watching, not wanting to startle her from her task. Her forehead puckered in concentration and her eyes narrowed. She blinked, and then I realized she was crying.

"Nan?" I moved to where she sat on the floor and squatted beside her. "What's wrong?"

Her expression switched from heartache to embarrassment. "Just felt like taking a trip down memory lane."

I looked down. Countless photographs lay scattered and spread inside the circular cardboard box. Black and white. Color. Faded. Dog-eared. Polaroid. Glossy prints. The box held just about every type of photo I could imagine as far as paper and media went, yet every picture contained the same thing. Family.

Most of the shots contained the same two people. Nan and Grandpa.

"I saw you leave the library," I said.

I'd been unsure whether or not I'd ever admit I knew her secret, but perhaps if she knew she had nothing to hide from me, she'd open up.

"I leave every night to walk home, Macaroon."

"Nice try." I sat beside her on the floor, crossing my legs as I plucked a photo from the box. In it, Grandpa sat at a table of trains, his grin as wide as that of a five-year-old on Christmas morning. "I watched you walk to the cemetery and sit by Grandpa's grave."

"How do you know it wasn't the first time I'd ever done that?"

I slung my arm around her shoulder and squeezed. "Face it. I'm on to you."

Nan blew out a sigh and took the photo from my fingers. "He loved those trains. Do you remember them?"

I nodded.

"Did you tell your mother you saw me?" Nan asked.

I shook my head. "Not a word."

"Good." Nan patted my knee. "She can be a little bossy in the grief-recovery department."

"No kidding. Don't even get me started on her fiancé-recovery techniques."

Our laughter built, mixing together and pushing aside Nan's tears.

We fell silent for several moments before I pointed to the photos. "Who took these?"

Nan ran her fingertips across the collection of photographs. "Your mother took most of them."

I reached out to touch a picture of my grandfather. The photo had captured the essence of the man I remembered so well, creating a lasting memory of his laughing eyes and crooked smile.

I flipped through several more shots, each capturing the personality of the moment, the photographer's skill evident.

Surprise washed through me. "Mom took these?"

Nan smiled. "I can remember a time when she was never without that camera of hers around her neck."

I, on the other hand, couldn't remember ever seeing my mother *with* a camera.

"What happened?" I asked.

Nan handed me two photos. "Life, Macaroon."

I dropped my focus to the captured images. In one black-and-white shot, my mother was young—all flowing hair, laughing smile, and carefree joy. Sure enough, a camera hung around her neck.

In the second photo, a Polaroid snapshot, my parents cradled a newborn me in their arms. My mother's smile was perfectly posed, an expression I knew all too well.

A wave of sadness threatened to overwhelm me.

"How far apart were these taken?" I asked.

Nan sighed. "About a year, give or take a month."

I pointed to the first picture and my mother's amazing expression. "Did she ever smile like that again?"

"Of course she did. She loves her family, Macaroon."

While I knew Nan was telling the truth, I couldn't help but stare at the picture of my carefree mother. In it, there was nothing posed; there was only genuine happiness.

"Who took this?" I asked.

"Your grandpa took that the day we gave her that camera."

I set the two photos back in the box, adding them to the countless others. "You have so many beautiful photos, Nan. Why don't you put these in an album?"

She hesitated before she answered, and when she spoke, raw emotion hung heavy in her words.

"These aren't pictures to be catalogued and forgotten on some shelf. These are memories."

I said nothing, letting the weight of her words settle inside me.

"These are all I have left," she added, her voice barely audible.

Then it hit me.

Just as I'd become shaped by expectations of my future, Nan had been shaped by memories of her past. The real question was whether or not we were both letting life pass us by while we focused on what might have been or on what once was.

I kissed the top of her head as I stood to leave, wanting to let her get back to memory lane.

"Take this, Macaroon." She pulled the carefree, happy photo of Mom from the box and handed it to me.

I froze momentarily, entranced by the sheer beauty of my mother's face. I held the snapshot gently as I stepped out into the hall. Then I walked into my room and slid it into a drawer, a treasure of the past and a reminder of how happy my mother had been when she hadn't been my mother at all.

I turned to study my own memories. Snapshots sat tucked into the corners of the mirror that hung above my bureau.

Photographs and ticket stubs covered the surface of my bulletin board, still holding the positions into which they'd been pinned more than a dozen years earlier.

There had been a time when I'd documented everything—significant and insignificant moments alike.

But were the insignificant moments really insignificant?

I scrambled across my bed, moving within inches of where the bulletin board hung on the wall. On it, countless faces smiled back at me in photos of middle school and high school memories captured for eternity.

A tug-of-war at the school picnic. A bathing-beauty shot at Paris's annual Parispalooza festival. A hug among best friends, determined to never lose touch.

Sure, the photos of awards night, senior prom, and graduation were there, but it was the other photos—the photos of the everyday moments—that brought back a rush of emotion. Those moments weren't insignificant at all...and they weren't boring. They were moments that mattered.

There had been a time when I'd gone everywhere with my camera in hand.

Nan's words about my mother and her camera echoed through my mind.

Had my mother been the same way?

After all, Mom had given me my secondhand Minolta at the start of senior year. She'd taught me everything I needed to know in order to add photography to my growing journalism skills. I'd gone on to document life at Paris High for the school newspaper and the yearbook.

I slid off my bed and opened my closet door, wondering where on earth I'd tucked the camera.

While other kids in my class had sported newfangled digital cameras, I'd carried the classic Minolta like the precious prize it was—a gift from my mother.

The camera had required thought, planning, and real film. I'd loved every moment.

I searched my brain for the last time I used it to take photographs, and my mind locked on the one night I'd worked so hard to forget.

I'd put away the Minolta the night the Paris Oak burned down. I hadn't touched it since.

I found the beauty tucked inside its black leather bag, braced against the wall of my closet between the chipped baseboard and a pair of forgotten snow boots.

I pulled out the bag and set it on my bed, running my hand across the dark, pebbled leather.

The zipper still stuck where it always had, about an inch and a half from the end of its run. I managed to pull the camera free just the same. It gleamed, the sight of it making my heart catch, and an odd flutter of excitement buzzed to life in my stomach.

I hurried back to the drawer where I'd tucked the photograph of Mom and compared the camera in my hand to the one that hung around her neck.

Identical.

My heart swelled with my new understanding of just how important this camera had been to her.

An idea swirled through my brain and lodged there.

I sank back onto the bed, cradling the Minolta in my lap.

Could I do for Mrs. O'Malley what my mother had done for Nan? Could I help her hold on to her memories?

You can't fix everything, Mick had said.

Maybe not.

But maybe, just maybe, I could help.

That night, in the final moments before I climbed into bed, I did not call Fred. As a matter of fact, I turned off my phone and set it on the far side of the bedroom.

I ran my hand across the Minolta's case and smiled at the photos on my bulletin board, seeing as if for the first time just how many of them included Mick. A shiver traced its way across my shoulders, and I pulled the covers up to my chin before snapping off the bedside lamp.

Moonlight spilled through the windows, distorting the shadows of my belongings, the mementos of my youth.

I couldn't help but wonder whether or not the shadows resembled the images inside Mrs. O'Malley's brain—distorted and just beyond reach.

Then I thought of Mick and how painful it must be to watch his mother slip away. Yet, after a lifetime of running, he'd come home.

A moonbeam bounced off the smattering of painted stars above my head, and I sighed. I studied the play of light against the iridescence, and then I did something I hadn't done in a long time.

I began to count.

CHAPTER FIFTEEN

— — —

I sat at the Paris River Café breakfast bar the next morning and stared at the estimate from Chuck Matthews.

"Nice hat," Jessica said as she refilled my coffee.

"I get a lot of that," I muttered, unable to rip my gaze from the sheet of paper's bottom line. I'd known the repairs would be extensive, but I hadn't been prepared for *this*.

Not covered by homeowner's insurance, I thought.

How in the hell was I ever going to pay for this? I had some money set aside for my honeymoon. Based on the continued lack of communication from Fred, I might have that cash available, but it still wouldn't be enough. Plus, the yellow Victorian was Fred's house as much as it was mine. Shouldn't he have a role in all this?

He was a man of integrity, I thought with a laugh. If I went ahead with the repairs, he'd surely help foot the bill. Of course, I'd also expected him to honor our wedding plans. Silly me.

Truth was, I had no idea of what he'd want anymore, but I wanted to fix the house. The question was how.

"You okay?" Jessica gave my forearm a quick shake, as if she'd been trying to get my attention and I hadn't heard a word.

"Yeah," I said out loud, even though I screamed *No way!* on the inside. "I'm fine."

"Is that Chuck's estimate?"

I nodded, carefully refolding the paper to make it fit back inside the envelope in which Chuck had delivered the news.

"Can I see it?" Jessica asked.

Her long blond hair hung straight today, with the top and sides anchored behind her head. I'd shoved my own hair up under the fedora, knowing I'd have a long day.

"Abby." Jessica gave me another shake. "Can I see it?" She reached for the envelope and then took it.

I read my scrawled name on the outside as Jessica slid out the sheet of paper and shook it open.

Too bad. For a moment, I'd hoped Chuck had given me someone else's project costs.

Jessica skimmed the piece of paper and swore. "Holy—"

"Hell," I said. "Holy hell."

My if-you-can't-say-anything-nice days were over.

I pressed my cheek to the cold, smooth counter and wished I could somehow transport myself back into the warm bed I'd left not even an hour earlier.

"Maybe we can get some of the materials ourselves," Jessica said. "Destiny's probably got tons of sources. And there's a great salvage yard just outside of town."

But my brain caught on one word in particular.

Destiny.

I straightened, thinking of how Destiny had mentioned work being slow.

What if I asked her to branch out from cabinetmaking? What if I convinced her to try a whole-house rescue?

She might say no. But maybe, just maybe, she'd say yes.

A few moments later, I burst out of the café's door and jogged down Artisan Alley.

Destiny's shop sat over a converted garage. The bottom area served as a small florist shop, while Destiny and her partner, Rock, worked upstairs.

The sun slanted between the trees, warming the look of the dark wood shingles that covered the entire building. Bright green shutters completed the effect, and I smiled at the sight of the front door, painted a brilliant violet that perfectly matched the stripe Destiny wore so blatantly and so proudly in her hair.

I climbed the wooden steps on the outside of the building, and a small wind chime sounded as I pushed through the door to the second floor. The smell of fresh coffee and doughnuts warmed the space—a crowded explosion of color and photographs, plans and worktables.

Rock looked up from the back of the space, his smile growing wide as he spotted me. "Cabby Abby," he called out. "Nice hat."

Such was the beauty of living in a small town like Paris. Nothing was sacred. Not even the nickname you'd been given by the town barber in the privacy of your own home.

I gave Rock a wave. "Nice haircut."

He jerked a thumb behind him. "She went in the back for some supplies. She'll be right out."

"What are you working on?" I asked Rock.

He pointed to a series of cabinets staged by the far wall. "New kitchen over on Fourth Avenue. We're custom matching the stain and installing them tomorrow."

I crossed to where the cabinets sat, running my hand across the gorgeous woodwork and the lush, satin finish.

"Have you guys ever done floors?"

"No." Destiny's voice startled me, but then she pulled me into a hug, which startled me more than her voice.

She took a step back, and I studied her momentarily, deciding to skip the chitchat and hit her with my idea.

"You should restore floors," I said. "My floors."

She hesitated, drawing a breath in through her nose. Rock stood up from his work area and busied himself as far away from us as he could.

"Sore subject?" I asked.

Destiny remained silent, doing nothing but breathing in and out. In and out.

"Feel free to answer me anytime at all," I said.

At that, she smiled. "Good sarcasm."

"I do my best."

Then she patted the cabinets beside me. "We do cabinets and furniture, Abby. I've never rehabbed a house."

"So why not start now?" I asked. "You told me business was slow. Just think of the before-and-after pictures we could take."

She'd twisted her long, dark hair up into a sloppy knot, and a pencil stuck out from behind one ear. Destiny had never wanted for an ounce of confidence, yet here she stood hesitating at the chance to tackle the renovation of my house.

"If you aren't interested in building up that area of your business, I understand."

"She's scared of it," Rock called out from the other side of the workshop.

I blinked, momentarily unable to wrap my brain around what he'd said. "Scared?" I narrowed my gaze on Destiny. "Since when are you scared of anything?"

"I'm good at small," she said. "I've never tried big."

"No time like the present." I reached into my pocket and pulled out the envelope from Chuck. "Just take a look. My guess is that you can do this. I have a little bit of savings, and maybe we can find some of the materials at salvage yards or something."

Destiny laughed. "Salvage yards? Who taught you that one?"

Hope spread through me. If she was laughing, maybe Destiny would go for my crazy idea—a discounted job in return for her first big showcase project.

"Jessica," I answered.

Destiny reached for the envelope, pulled out the estimate sheet, and shook it open. Her dark brows furrowed, but then they lifted. When she smiled, I knew she'd made up her mind.

I'd never seen or heard Destiny worry about the future or analyze the past. She lived her life. Plain and simple. No pretense. No bullshit.

"Do you think we could be more opposite?" I asked.

"You think too much." She hooked her arm through my elbow and steered me to a clean workspace.

"Rock," she called out, "grab the doughnuts and pull up a chair. Let's look at this bid and then head over to Second Avenue. Maybe it's time we tried rehabbing a house."

Mick was painting the front steps of his mother's house when I got home.

"I passed on Chuck's estimate," I said as I stood to the side of where he worked.

He looked up at me, his dark brows lifting in question.

"I went to see Destiny instead."

His brows furrowed. "Destiny?"

I nodded. "She's an amazing carpenter. Why not let her try to fix this?"

"Because it's your house." He dropped his focus back to his work.

"You won't believe how thorough she was," I continued. "She and Rock not only found a larger area of damage up in the joists, but they showed me a section of living room wall that has to go."

Mick smiled without looking up. "Listen to you. If I didn't know better, I'd think you've learned a thing or two."

He visibly concentrated on his brushstrokes, smoothing fresh white paint across the risers of the home's front porch steps.

As I watched Mick work, I thought about the photos tacked to the bulletin board in my old bedroom.

His features, circumstances, and life had changed, but deep inside he was still Mick. He was still my friend.

"Need some help?" I asked.

Mick looked up at me, smiled, and did something completely out of character. He said yes.

"There's a spare brush over by the tray." He pointed with his elbow.

I took off Dad's fedora, pushed up my sleeves, and helped Mick paint. We worked side by side, brushing a fresh color over the top of the stripped, sanded wood beneath.

Part of me wondered if somewhere deep inside Mick didn't wish his mother's brain were as easy to restore as the steps.

I kept my thoughts to myself, though, staying quiet, knowing exactly how Mick liked to work.

But as the afternoon grew longer, and the sun began to slide in the sky, I broke my silence one last time.

"Hey, Mick? Does your mom like dogs?"

CHAPTER SIXTEEN

—— —— ——

Don Michaels and Riley arrived midafternoon on Tuesday for
their first visit with Mrs. O'Malley.

I'd tracked Don down through the Widow Murphy's nephew,
her only living relative. He'd given me the number for the orga-
nization where Don and Riley volunteered. They'd only been too
happy to put Mrs. O'Malley on their visit schedule.

The day was warm, and the wild cherry tree in the O'Malley's
side yard had burst into bloom. We sat beneath its shade and
sweet aroma, settling into the folding chairs Mick had brought up
from the basement.

Mick had already excused himself, looking uncomfortable
with the extra company, when Frankie emerged through the gap
in the hedges.

She'd pulled her black hair into a severe ponytail and, based
on her rapid breathing, she'd most likely jogged home from school
to get here as early as she had. She'd been nervous about today's
visit ever since we'd made the plans. I knew she was only being
protective of Mrs. O'Malley, but I hoped she'd warm to the idea of
using pet therapy as much as I had.

Frankie's guitar brushed against the fabric of her skinny
black jeans as she came to a stop. She frowned as she sank into

an empty chair, and I reached over to pat her knee. "Tough day at the office?"

She dodged my touch, saying nothing as she cut her eyes from me to Don and then to Riley. She reached for Mrs. O'Malley, letting her hand come to rest on the arm of the older woman's folding chair.

I quickly introduced Frankie to Don and Riley, then watched Detta O'Malley brighten as Riley sat beside her.

He wiggled in against the hem of Detta's skirt, and when she reached to scratch his head, he rewarded her efforts with a slurp of her fingertips.

Detta's pale cheeks flushed with color, but Frankie's features tensed and held, her every muscle wound as tight as one of her guitar strings.

I stroked the camera case in my lap, unhooking the magnetic snaps that held the back shut. I'd located a roll of film at Ted Miller's pharmacy and sat ready, waiting to capture today's memories for Detta.

Yet, instead of clicking off shots of Detta's first moments with Riley, I remained focused on my sister's obvious discomfort.

Mrs. O'Malley giggled, and Frankie looked away.

And then it hit me.

My sister was hurt.

Don and I exchanged a glance. He smiled and mouthed the word *watch*.

Without a word of direction, Riley shifted his focus to Frankie. His black ears pricked to attention, and he tipped his head to one side.

The dog gave Detta's hand a quick lick before he left her side to trot over to Frankie's chair.

Instead of sitting beside her, as he'd done with Detta, he put one tentative paw on Frankie's knee. Without waiting for permission or admonition, he pushed upward, standing on his back legs with both front paws planted squarely in my sister's lap.

Frankie sat back, her expression startled yet amused.

Riley moved with lightning speed, licking her chin before she had a chance to turn away, react, or flee the scene.

Then Frankie smiled.

She uttered the dog's name in soft protest, but her arm came around Riley's neck as he settled against her.

I leaned toward Don and whispered, "Do therapy dogs typically climb up on the patients they visit?"

He shook his head and gave me a quick wink. "He knows better."

I narrowed my eyes.

"Riley knows Frankie's not sick." He dropped his voice low. "She just needs reassurance."

Who didn't need reassurance when they were fifteen?

Riley settled between Frankie and Detta, and the two friends—the teen with her whole life ahead of her and the woman whose life was slowly fading away—smiled at each other over the top of the dog's head.

Don repositioned his chair, scooting closer to the small group. He pointed to Frankie's guitar.

"Do you play?" he asked.

Frankie's protective mask slid back into place. "A little."

"*Would* you play?" Don asked when it became apparent Frankie wasn't going to pick up her guitar without an additional push.

Frankie studied Don carefully, then she gave the fur between Riley's ears one more scratch and glanced at Detta.

Mrs. O'Malley smiled at the dog, mesmerized by his presence.

My sister typically played in the privacy of her room or alone with Detta. Don's question put her on the spot and made her visibly uncomfortable.

She studied Detta, Riley, and then Detta once more. Then she smiled, a tentative grin that infused me with pride and hope.

"Okay." Frankie shrugged, sliding her aloofness securely in place. "Maybe one song."

She pulled her guitar onto her lap, checked the strings, and began. I slipped the case off my camera and adjusted the aperture and distance settings, just as I'd done back in my youth.

As Frankie's soft melody rose into the air above the O'Malleys' backyard, I took my first shot and then my second.

When Detta's voice rang out, happy and sure, her melody intertwined with the guitar's chords, I clicked off my third shot and then my fourth.

Frankie beamed as if illuminated by the music. Detta smiled as she sang freely, beautifully. Riley settled in the grass at their feet, his white-tipped tail gently wagging.

I captured every moment, slipping out of my chair to change my position and camera angle, snapping photos until I could advance the film no further.

As for Frankie, her inner beauty and passion flowed from her fingertips to the guitar as she played, her notes becoming one with Mrs. O'Malley's voice. Any sign of hesitancy or the need for reassurance had vanished, leaving behind a teenager happily lost in her music.

Nan appeared a short while later, wielding a dish of freshly baked oatmeal cookies. The afternoon had gone chilly, and she'd slipped into one of Grandpa's favorite cardigan sweaters. I'd told her about Detta's special visitors, and she'd insisted on bringing over a snack.

Don rose from his chair as she approached, and Nan's steps faltered.

An odd moment passed between them before Don reached for the plate and gestured for Nan to take his seat.

"Have you two met?" I asked, pushing to my feet.

Both shook their heads, and Don said, "Won't you please join us?"

His features brightened and he pulled himself taller, a definite sparkle of attraction humming to life in his gaze.

As I made the introductions, I imagined how my grandmother must look through the eyes of a stranger, through the eyes of Don Michaels, a widower of similar age.

Nan was beautiful—stunning, actually—inside and out.

As she thanked Don for the seat, a flush of soft pink blossomed in her cheeks.

Yet in her eyes lurked one unmistakable emotion, and my heart gave a sympathetic pang.

Nan's gaze shone full of fear, as if she might bolt and run at any moment. But she didn't, and I was thankful.

Instead, she joined our small group and stayed. My grandmother never fully relaxed in Don's presence, but as the afternoon sun slipped, we sat together—five humans and one canine—in comfortable companionship.

We sang songs. We ate cookies. We settled into one another's company and created a memory together.

I could only hope the pictures I'd taken would help Detta keep that memory as her own.

CHAPTER SEVENTEEN

—— —— ——

I walked along the streets of Paris, gazing longingly into shop window after shop window, my fingertips trailing across the glass and stone, my feet working for balance atop the cobblestones.

The Eiffel Tower loomed in the distance, visible in glimpses from alleyways and turned corners, like a ghost hovering above the city.

This was not the Paris of my home, but rather the Paris of my dreams. The *real* Paris. The Paris Fred had chosen over me.

But even so, the sound of my laughter rose through the early morning mist, teasing at the still, quiet air.

The myriad scents from a nearby bakery beckoned to me, their tendrils reaching out with the promise of warmth, cinnamon, and yeast.

My stomach growled, an intrusion into the land of my sleep. I willed myself to stay in the place my subconscious had conjured.

My mouth watered, and I hesitated at the bakery entrance, tentatively turning the gleaming brass knob as I pushed against the bright blue door.

I eased inside, expecting to find the space alive with activity—bakers bustling about, bread rising, pastries cooling. I found darkness instead, nothing more than an empty hollow of a store, cold and dark.

A chill swept through me, and I stepped backward, through the blue door and onto the street.

"Abby," a voice called out.

I blinked, not quite sure whether the voice originated from the bakery or from somewhere beyond the street on which I stood.

I retraced my steps, peered through the door once more, and gasped. My breath caught in my lungs and burned.

Fred stood before me, his face pale, his features set.

"Fred?" I asked.

But he said nothing. He did nothing. He made no effort to return my greeting.

A brightness illuminated the air behind me, and I turned away from Fred's silent image, searching elsewhere, following the expanse of street behind me in search of the light.

The sun, I surmised. Surely nothing more than the morning sun making its appearance.

"Abby," a voice called out, this voice different, deeper, stronger.

But this time, unlike the first time, I felt no uncertainty. Without hesitation, I knew where to look, where to turn.

A man's silhouette emerged from behind the morning mist, rounding the corner, reaching out a hand to me.

The morning sun brightened, chasing away all remaining hints of shadow. The stranger's face became one I'd known for most of my life.

"Abby?" he repeated, waiting for my response.

I said nothing, unable to push past my surprise and confusion, even though I felt a calm assurance, as if I'd known this moment might come one day.

Mick.

But then he was gone—vanished as if he'd never really stood before me at all.

I blinked my eyes open and stared at the wall of my bedroom. My heart pounded in my chest as if I'd run a marathon or had a shock.

A shock, I thought. *Most definitely a shock.*

I fumbled my way into the bathroom, splashing water on my face. Even so, the smell of the Parisian bakery stayed with me. As a matter of fact, the scents of yeast and cinnamon had grown stronger, as if they came from inside my parents' house.

Back in my bedroom, I slid my feet into my clogs, pulled a sweatshirt over my nightgown, and glanced at my cell phone. Five thirty in the morning.

I stood in my open bedroom door and listened. The house was silent, evidence of the fact that most everyone else still slept.

Then from downstairs, I heard the sound of ceramic against granite, followed by the squeak of the oven door as it opened and closed.

I made my way down the steps as silently as I could, years of practice guiding me around the creaks intrinsic to hundred-year-old wood.

One, two, step to the left. Three, step wide to the right. Four, step left. Five, six, dead center, and so on, until I eased to the bottom.

Whoever was in the kitchen hummed softly. I suspected that person was not my mother, who had never carried a tune—hummed, sung, or otherwise—in her life.

I rounded the kitchen door half expecting to find Nan in the kitchen, unable to sleep, yet whoever hummed and rattled around sounded far more like…

Buddy Halladay. My father.

"What are you doing?" I asked.

I admit I might have tried a softer approach, but dropping the spoon and clutching his chest was a bit much, even for Dad.

"Abigail." He staggered backward. "What are you doing?"

"I asked you first."

I closed the space between us, taking note of the dusting of flour across the granite counter, the cracked eggshells in the sink, and the flowered, ruffled apron he'd tied around his waist.

"Are you baking?" I asked.

Dad shifted his eyes to the ceiling, a sure sign that whatever he was about to say was less than 100 percent true. "Your mother asked me to keep an eye on things while she…"

"Sleeps like a log upstairs?"

He met my disbelieving glare and sighed. "Something like that."

"I take it you've done this before?" I pointed to the pan of cinnamon buns resting on the counter.

Dad nodded. "Usually not this early. I usually do the setup and leave." The full ramifications of my father's words hit me, and I took a backward step.

Dad said nothing. Instead, he turned, placed a plate flat over the pan of pastries, and expertly flipped them. He lifted the pan clear, holding it steady as warm, caramel-colored syrup streamed off the edges, dripping down to coat the rolls below.

"You do the baking?" My voice had gone flat with disbelief. "And Mom takes the credit?"

He shrugged. "Everyone knows she can't cook, but they think she can do this. Let her have this one thing, Abby."

He set the pan in the sink and hoisted the plate in my direction. "Cinnamon roll?"

I considered reminding him about the perils of deceiving your children, but after a quick mental toss-up between the lecture and the cinnamon rolls, I chose the latter.

I had my priorities, after all.

"I'll make the coffee," I said.

Dad nodded. "I'll grab the napkins."

So there we sat, sharing cinnamon rolls before dawn in the kitchen where I'd spent my entire life believing my mother to be some sort of idiot savant in the kitchen—a woman incapable of preparing an edible meal yet gifted beyond words when it came to melt-in-your-mouth pastries, cakes, and pies.

I realized that sometimes the things you held as absolute fact weren't fact at all, and sometimes that was all right.

I found it rather sweet, actually, that Dad baked for Mom.

But then I thought about something else he'd said.

I usually do the setup and leave.

"Where do you go when you leave?"

Dad looked at me blankly.

"On my bike," I said. "Where do you go?"

He gave me a slight shrug, as if the answer was obvious. "I ride, Abby. I'm fifty years old. You'll see someday. Exercise is important."

I shook my head. "Do you honestly think I believe that?"

He studied me then, a smile pulling at the corners of his mouth. "No," he answered.

"So are you going to tell me the truth?"

Dad shook his head. "Someday, maybe. Not today."

Disappointment rolled through me, but I respected his answer. *Someday* was better than never. And maybe *someday* would come sooner than I thought.

We each polished off one more roll before I waddled back to bed, needing a few more hours of sleep before I donned Dad's fedora and started my rounds.

CHAPTER EIGHTEEN

—— —— ——

I spent the day driving fares between Paris and Trenton. I'd settled into a pattern that had not only become comfortable but also afforded me time to think.

I hadn't decided if that was a good thing or not.

The images from my dream remained sharply focused in my brain, and the downtime between fares gave me plenty of opportunity for psychoanalyzing myself.

What the hell was I doing dreaming about Mick?

Luckily, my cell phone rang just in time to interrupt my latest deep thoughts.

I pressed the button on my Bluetooth, smiling when I heard the excitement in Destiny's voice.

"We're ready for you," she said. "How soon can you come by the house?"

I was fifteen minutes outside of town in light traffic. "Twenty minutes."

"See you then."

I knew Destiny and Rock had begun demolition on the damaged areas of my house that morning. We'd settled on a price I could afford, and our plan was to find the materials we'd need at a discounted cost.

Demolition.

Just the sound of the word gave me chills.

But when I arrived at the house, the scene was even worse than I'd imagined.

Much of the living room floor was missing, the wide pine planks I'd fallen in love with gone, ripped from where they'd once been the crowning beauty of the first floor.

The wide molding was shredded, and Rock worked at cutting away wallboard, exposing the damaged studs and support pieces.

I stared at what was left of the home Fred and I had bought as-is and thought only one thing. Nothing about this scene would fall in the assets column on Fred's ledger sheets.

"You okay?" Destiny asked. "You look a little pale."

"I guess I hadn't realized it would look so—"

"Terrifying?" she asked. "This is the worst it will be." Then she laughed. "If you're freaked out by this, don't even think about going down to the basement."

She led me over to a makeshift workbench where she'd spread out notes, diagrams, and blueprints for the areas to be replaced and restored.

As she spoke, her words swirled around my brain, not fully registering. While I appreciated her enthusiasm and her obvious preparation, the magnitude of the job left me shaken. I began to wonder if I'd made a mistake by talking Destiny into taking on my house.

I pivoted slowly, taking in the full effect of the ripped-up pine planks and the portions of wall in which everything but the studs and framing had been stripped away. The radiators sat disconnected and lined up against the kitchen wall, and I knew the basement held the horror of damaged beams and joists.

"It's so much," I said, failing miserably at hiding my dismay at the state of the house.

Destiny nodded slowly, the lines of worry unmistakable around her eyes. "Focus on how great your house is going to look after we're done."

A wave of sadness washed through me, pushing aside my concerns about Destiny's abilities.

I could picture how beautiful the finished product would be, but the truth was, I wasn't sure I'd be the one living in the house. I still hadn't heard from Fred, so who knew if he was ever coming back?

I'd contacted his parents, who had told me that their son was safe, happy, and needed to be left alone. The Newtons had never been the warm and fuzzy sort, but even for them, their response had been a bit harsh.

I snapped myself back to reality.

"You do know I may not be able to afford to stay here even if I can find a way to get the materials for repairs."

Destiny nodded. "It'll all work out the way it's supposed to."

I squinted at her. "You're not going soft on me, are you?"

Destiny stepped close and grasped my shoulders. "Are we friends?"

I nodded.

"Do you trust me?"

"You're the most painfully honest person I know," I said.

She laughed. "Then relax."

Emotion lodged in my throat, and I dropped my gaze to what remained of my home's once-beautiful floor. Tears filled my eyes and I squeezed them shut.

Much to my astonishment, Destiny wrapped me in her arms and held on tight until I calmed down. Then, she held me out to arm's length and brushed my hair out of my face. In her eyes, I saw a kindness and love that only a true friend could offer.

And then she said, "Now get the hell out before you get your tears all over what little floor we have left."

∽

Fortunately for me, Miller's Apothecary owned a machine capable of printing good, old-fashioned photographs.

Unfortunately for me, Ted Miller felt compelled to enlighten me with his wisdom the entire time I waited there on my way home.

I'd dropped off the film on my way out of town that morning, hoping to be able to avoid Ted when I came back to pick up prints. No such luck.

Ted, who apparently had nothing better to do with his time, said he hadn't been able to stop thinking about my job predicament. Even more astonishing was the fact he'd hit upon the solution to all my problems—a new career as a pharmacy technician.

While I had nothing against either pharmacists or their technicians, I did have an aversion to working with Ted. Listening to him was bad enough. Working with him would require me to be either a masochist or deaf.

As he blathered on and I ignored him completely, I realized that during the past hour with Destiny, some of her honesty had rubbed off.

My thoughts on my so-called conversation with Ted were anything but nice. As a matter of fact, my thoughts were blunt. Painfully blunt.

When Ted launched into an extended diatribe on the definition of edgy as it applied to syndicated columns, and how I would never achieve edgy or a syndicated column, I decided the time had come to channel my inner Destiny.

"I find your conversation tiresome and rude, Ted."

Ted Miller blinked. His mouth opened, but no additional words came out. I gave myself a mental high five, even though I knew I'd been less than kind.

When he regained his composure and launched into additional thoughts on my communications ability, I thought about saying shut up. But I didn't say it. I wasn't quite ready to be that rude to someone's face.

I did, however, hold up my hand in the universal sign for will-you-please-stop-talking-now-for-the-love-of-all-that-is-holy?

When his photography technician announced that my prints were done, I slapped down my cash and left without saying good-bye.

I drove home feeling proud of myself, albeit guilty, for my behavior.

When I walked through the kitchen door five minutes later, my mother turned to face me, crossing her arms and raising one brow.

Nan stood behind Mom's back and gave me the thumbs-up sign. "Macaroon, no matter what your mother says, I'm glad you stood up to the blowhard."

"Who?" I asked, pulling my stack of prints out of their cardboard sleeve.

"Ted. Miller." My mother spoke the name slowly, as if fashioning two distinct sentences from the man's name. I might be thirty years old, but apparently "my house, my rules" had no statute of limitations.

Even for Paris, news of my transgression had spread at record speed.

"Sorry, Mom. I couldn't take it anymore."

She hesitated for a beat, and Nan made her move. "What have you got there?"

"The pictures from Don and Riley's visit."

Mom said nothing more about my remarks to Ted, so I shifted my attention to the stack of prints. I flipped through the photos, studying each shot and realizing they were not the memory-capturing masterpieces I'd imagined they would be.

Far from it.

The photos were just that. *Photos.* I'd failed to capture the importance of Don and Riley's visit. Somehow, I'd missed the mark.

There were shots of Frankie, sure. But they were nothing more than pictures of a young woman playing a guitar. They failed to communicate how it had felt to witness the blend of Frankie's music and Detta's voice, and how Frankie had beamed as she strummed her guitar.

"It's a good start, honey," Mom said over my shoulder.

I blew out a slow breath. "What do you mean?" Although I knew exactly what she meant.

She tapped a group shot of Frankie, Detta, and Riley, pointing to the scenery. "Your composition and lighting are excellent, but you need to capture the heart of the shot. Keep trying."

I thought of her photo, hidden upstairs in my bedroom, and understood exactly what she meant. When Grandpa had taken the shot, he'd seen her pure elation and joyful spirit and had preserved her emotion forever with the click of a camera's shutter.

What had she called it? *The heart of the shot?*

"How do you know so much about photography?" I asked, testing to see how much information she'd volunteer.

Mom offered nothing but a shrug. "I really don't," she answered. "Just making a suggestion."

Nan said nothing, standing by quietly, watching as Mom slid the stack of photos out of my hands and flipped through the images, one by one.

Finally Mom paused, setting aside a picture of Don.

In the shot, he rested his chin on his fists, apparently unaware I'd taken his photo.

His focus fell not on Detta, or Riley, or Frankie, but on a point somewhere beyond the camera's field of vision. Attraction, however, shone clearly in the set of his features and the softness of his gaze.

"That's emotion." Mom tapped the print. "What was he looking at?"

I released a soft laugh. "Not what...who."

Nan cleared her throat and headed for the center hall, fleeing the kitchen before I said another word.

"Who?" Mom asked.

I pointed to the empty spot where Nan had just stood. "He was watching Nan."

Mom turned the print to get a better look before she smiled and nodded. "That's interesting. Very interesting."

And as usual, she was right...again.

CHAPTER NINETEEN

A flash of color in my parents' front flower bed captured my attention as I set out the next morning to cruise the streets of Paris in the Beast.

I slowed the monster cab, confusion twisting my gut with a slight flip. Someone was in the garden. Why?

And then I saw the intruder more fully. Detta O'Malley.

I pulled the Beast to a stop and cut the ignition.

"Detta?" I crossed the front lawn as quickly as I could, anxiety tripping inside me. Was she hurt? Confused? Ill?

A handful of yellow tulip petals fluttered up into the air from where Mrs. O'Malley sat bent over in the middle of my mother's prizewinning garden.

"Mrs. O'Malley?"

I reached for her elbow, but she pushed me away, her reaction speed and strength both taking me by surprise.

I sat back on my haunches to put a bit of space between us. "Mrs. O'Malley," I repeated more softly. "What are you doing?"

"Weeding," she answered. "I have to pull these weeds." A second handful of plants flew—my mother's prized peach tulips, if I wasn't mistaken.

"Mrs. O'Malley." I worked to keep my tone gentle. While I didn't want to frighten her, I had to stop her before she destroyed my mother's entire flower bed. "These aren't weeds."

I reached for her again, tugging lightly at her arm. This time she pulled free and moved sideways, away from me.

I scrambled to my feet and headed for the front door, calling out as I flung the door open, "Frankie! I need you out front."

Back in the garden, Mrs. O'Malley had moved on to Mom's ivory, pink, and red tulips, last year's first-place winner in the Paris Garden Club theme competition. All that remained was a scattered mess of petals and leaves, trampled and plucked from the earth.

Mom appeared at the opened front door, her pansy-print apron now tied neatly around her waist instead of Dad's.

Frankie stumbled out from behind her, wiping sleep from her eyes. Missy barreled past them both, gleefully raising her hands at the sight of petals floating on the morning breeze.

"Confetti!" she hollered, dancing down the steps to twist and turn in the pile of discarded flowers.

My mother paled and Frankie's eyes widened. "Detta," they both said in unison.

"I tried to stop her." My words sounded lame and ineffective. I looked from my family to Detta and back again.

Frankie reached the garden first, gently snaking one arm around Mrs. O'Malley's waist. "Morning, Detta. Want to come sit with me?"

I found my sister's calm composure humbling. Her love for Mick's mother lit my sister from within. Never was that more apparent than in that moment.

"I have to pull these weeds," Detta said, frustration evident in her tone. "I have to pull these weeds."

I glanced at my mother, who moved slowly, descending the front porch steps at a snail's pace, as if gathering her thoughts and formulating her plan of action as she went.

Her expression shifted from one of horror to one of compassion as she neared. Then she knelt beside Frankie and Mrs. O'Malley.

"I have to pull these weeds," Detta repeated.

My mother wiped her hands on her apron and brushed an invisible hair from her eyes. "Where shall we start?"

Frankie and I exchanged puzzled glances. Mrs. O'Malley pointed to an untouched bed of lavender-tipped blossoms.

My mother swallowed, but as her throat visibly worked, her eyes shimmered with kindness. "Let's get to work."

Frankie and I sat in stunned silence momentarily. I could barely believe my ears. Mom had just declared war on the garden she loved and nurtured as if it were a fourth child.

As Missy danced and twirled, spinning freely across the front yard with youthful abandon, Mrs. O'Malley instructed the rest of us on what to pull and where.

I saw something in Detta O'Malley's eyes I hadn't seen since I'd first found her, standing beside the curb on Bridge Street, cradling a dead spider plant in her arms.

Purpose.

While my initial reaction had been to correct Mick's mother, Mom's reaction had been to encourage her. Instead of saving the garden, my mother had chosen to let Detta have this small moment in which she felt control.

In that instant, there were no worries about appearances or memory loss. There was simply the moment—a moment in which we pulled apart a garden in order to let Detta know her wishes still mattered.

"I'll be right back," I said.

I raced inside and up the stairs to my room, snagging the old Minolta from where I'd last set it down. Then I returned to the front garden to document the desecration of Madeline Halladay's award-winning tulips.

Just as I'd done in the O'Malleys' backyard, I adjusted the settings for light and distance before I took my shots. I captured the barren earth, the upturned roots, the pile of discarded greens, and the smiles on the face of each female as she worked.

But this time, unlike the photos I'd taken earlier in the week, I shifted my focus from images to feelings.

I immersed myself in the emotion of the moment and let it guide me as I clicked off frame after frame of the scene before me.

I captured Mom's kindness, Frankie's warmth, and Detta's purpose.

Yes, I captured the flare of Missy's skirt as she twirled across the yard, but I also captured the way that spontaneous, once-in-a-lifetime moment made each of us *feel*.

The moment mattered. Our emotions mattered.

And in understanding those two truths, I discovered a purpose all my own.

CHAPTER TWENTY

— — —

I set out that morning with an idea that started a fire within me like none I'd ever known.

Images of the town I'd loved all my life swirled through my mind's eye as I turned the Beast from Front Street onto Bridge. Shopkeepers swept the cobblestones in front of their storefronts and waved as I passed.

I waved back, tipping Dad's fedora and wondering what *moment* would matter most to each of them that day. Would Manny, the barber, spend his day worrying about whether he'd make this month's rent, or would he go home tonight warmed by the memory of a child's smile after a first haircut?

Would Polly down at the Clip and Curl spend every minute wondering why she hadn't moved to the empty storefront over on Race Street when she had the chance, or would she lose herself in the laughter of her clients, knowing that while they sat in her chair, they felt like queens?

And what about me? Maybe today would be the day I stopped obsessing over what might have been and started focusing on what was right in front of me.

Paris.

I spotted Mona Capshaw on the corner of Front and First.

She sagged beneath two overstuffed tote bags—one slung over each shoulder—even as she balanced a large box in her arm.

I pulled Bessie to the curb and leaned to crank down the passenger window. "Want a lift?" I asked. "On the house."

"Argh," she said, and I instantly questioned my selection of passenger. I'd completely forgotten about today's Clipper meeting.

I scrambled out of the cab and around to the curb, pulling open the back door as I helped Mona place the box and totes inside on the large bench seat.

"Headed to Jessica's?" I asked.

"Argh," she answered.

I did a mental eye roll. "Ever say anything other than 'argh,' Mona?"

"Argh." Her pale-blue eyes glimmered with amusement.

"That's what I thought." I laughed.

"Does Buddy know you're giving away free rides?" Mona asked a few moments later as we rounded the turn toward her granddaughter's restaurant.

I shook my head and wondered what my father would think of my latest idea. "I have a feeling he's not that concerned about the cab these days."

"And what about you?" she asked. "You have any plans other than cruising around all day in your father's fedora?"

I grinned and hoisted the old Minolta from its place on the seat beside me. "I'm going back to real journalism." I hesitated for a split second, choosing my next words carefully. "And life moments."

Mona fell silent as I pulled the cab to a stop next to the Paris Café.

She leaned over the seat back between us. "What do you mean, life moments?"

"Life moments." I gave a quick shrug then shucked the camera free of its leather case. "How about today, for example? What's been your favorite life moment of today?"

Mona frowned. "You mean memory?"

I gave another shrug. "You could call it that." I gestured with one hand as I steadied the camera with the other. "But I'm talking about the simple moments. The instants that make each day special, even though we usually don't give them the credit they deserve."

Her frown deepened. "You may be spending too much time inside this cab."

I laughed and aimed the camera at her scowl, focusing the lens as if I knew what I was doing. "What was your favorite part of today?"

I expected to hear something about getting ready for the Clipper meeting, or about her work down at the community gardens, but her answer took me completely by surprise.

"I woke up."

I blinked. Then a bubble of warmth burst inside me.

Mona Capshaw's answer was so perfect in its simplicity, I couldn't think of a better way to start my new project.

Mona's expression softened and she smiled. "Hell," she said, "I'm not getting any younger."

I snapped off the shot, capturing the moment in which she laughed at her own words; then I flipped open the small writing tablet I'd found in a kitchen drawer and made my first entry.

Mona Capshaw. "I woke up."

I helped Mona carry her Clipper paraphernalia into the restaurant, and she grasped my hand and gave it a quick squeeze.

"You know," she said with an uncharacteristic softness that left me more than a little unnerved, "you're more like your mother every day."

I glanced down at my jeans and sweatshirt, touched a hand to my dad's hat, and frowned.

I was quite certain my mother wouldn't be caught dead looking like this. Surely Mona couldn't be serious.

She patted my arm. "It's a good thing. You'll see."

The Clipper crowd seemed larger than I remembered, and in the middle of the gathering Jessica and Destiny huddled together, deep in conversation, their features even more animated than usual.

"Big crowd today," I said as I set down Mona's box.

"I keep telling you to give clipping a try." Mona snapped her fingers. Excitement danced in her eyes. "Grab your camera."

"For what?"

She gestured dramatically to the group of Clippers behind her. "For this."

I laughed, realizing she was absolutely correct. This was a moment.

I dashed out to the cab, grabbed my camera, and rushed back inside.

Mona had gathered the Clippers into a tight group. There they sat—neighbors, friends, family—all waiting to have their picture taken by me.

"It's a bit like herding cats," Mona called out, and the entire group burst into laughter.

I clicked off a quick shot, then three more, before someone yelled, "Are we clipping coupons or posing for portraits?"

As the group dispersed and I turned to leave, Mona reached for my elbow, stopping me in my tracks.

"Thank you, Abby."

I blinked back the moisture that had suddenly blurred my vision and gave the older woman a hug. From across the room, Destiny winked.

Then a flash of color from across the street captured my attention.

Pink.

My pink.

My pink Schwinn.

I gave the Clippers a wave and a smile and broke into a jog, focused only on reaching the Beast as quickly as possible.

CHAPTER TWENTY-ONE

Dad handled the old pink Schwinn like a pro as he emerged from the alley next to Johnny's Test Kitchen and headed toward Race Street.

He made a left just as I jumped inside the Beast and cranked on the ignition. I was about to attempt a covert tail while driving a bright yellow classic cab as big as a small school bus. Who was I kidding?

Fortunately, there were no rearview mirrors on the bike. Unfortunately, Dad moved pretty well for a middle-aged guy.

He zipped along Race Street, headed for Bridge. In all likelihood, he'd make a right on Front and then another right on Third, toward home.

Surprise filled me when he reached the end of the street and turned left just before he hit the river, heading south on Front.

I slowed Bessie to a stop and signaled a left turn.

My father stood on the opposite corner, the bike parked beside him. He stared directly at the cab, hands fisted on his hips, dark brows lifted toward his still-full head of hair.

So much for my covert abilities. Of course, I'd never fully mastered that skill set.

I flashed back on countless nights Dad had adopted the same pose, standing on our front porch as I tried to sneak in after curfew.

Exhaling slowly, I made the turn and pulled the Beast to the curb. I cut the ignition and leaned across the seat to roll down the passenger window. "Dad? What are you doing here?" I said, doing my best to feign innocence.

He raised one hand and crooked his finger.

Fueled by the knowledge that he was the one who needed to do some explaining and not me, I slid across the seat and climbed out onto the curb.

The midafternoon sun beat down, doing nothing to abate the shiver that slid through me nonetheless at the thought of confronting Dad.

"Well?" I said, taking the offensive.

He pointed at me, and I spotted the flash of Irish temper in the color of his cheeks. "Well, yourself." He took a quick pace to one side and then back again. "Is that any way to drive Bessie? It's a wonder you haven't been pulled over for reckless endangerment."

I thought about backing down, but instead refocused on the task at hand.

"Oh, no you don't." I pointed at *him*. "What were you doing, zipping through downtown Paris on my old bike?"

He narrowed his eyes. "I've been thinking about painting her a new color."

"Not the point, Dad. Where have you been going every morning?" I threw my arms up in the air as I spoke. Two could play the Irish-temper game. "And don't say *exercise*."

"Abigail Marie," he said. "There are some things that are a man's business and his private business alone."

"Dad"—I closed the space between us—"your *little* rides last for hours." I leaned close and gave him a good sniff. "What is that smell?"

The Buddy Halladay lack-of-poker-face phenomenon was in full effect. "Rosemary?" He said the word as if asking a question. "Maybe basil?"

And then I realized the answer to where Dad had been going every morning had been percolating in my brain all along.

"Have you been cooking?" I asked.

He nodded.

"Cooking?" I repeated. And then the puzzle pieces snapped into place. "At the new restaurant? Johnny's?"

Dad nodded. "I help with the breakfast crowds."

He walked toward the bike and pulled an oblong brown bag from the basket. Then he headed for a bench, sat, and patted the slats beside him.

"What is that?" I asked.

"Turkey, provolone, roast beef, Jersey tomatoes, and…"

"Rosemary and basil?"

He nodded. "That young man from New York can make one hell of a sandwich. He's taught me a lot."

I thought of my conversations with Jessica and her fears about losing business to Johnny's Test Kitchen.

"Good food fast?" I asked.

Another nod. "He understands what people want. Everyone's in a hurry." Dad shrugged. "Why not cater to them?"

I sat beside him and clasped my hands in my lap out of frustration. "Why would you keep this a secret?"

Dad placed his hands on top of mine and held on tight.

"The first time I took out your bike, I really was just going for a ride. I figured, I'm not so busy now, I should get in shape." He shrugged. "I rode a few miles, then checked out the new restaurant for breakfast."

I shook my head. "Instead of Jessica's?"

Dad's gaze softened. "There's plenty of room in Paris for two restaurants."

He was probably right, but that didn't answer my main question. "How on earth did you start cooking for him?"

"A long time ago, I had a summer job as a short-order cook. I loved that job." He laughed.

"When I saw how busy Johnny was, I offered to step in. Just for that morning." He waved his hand dismissively. "But I've been going back ever since."

My dad. A short-order cook.

His eyes shimmered as he told me the story, and I realized he loved being in the kitchen. Cooking made him happy. Didn't we all deserve to do the thing that made us happy?

"It was something I always wanted to do," he continued. "But once I took over Halladay Cabs, I set that aside."

"But now you have time," I said.

"Now I have time." He bumped his shoulder against mine. "And I can make one hell of an omelet."

Having tasted my dad's baking, I had no doubt he was killer with a spatula. "But why didn't you tell anybody?"

Dad shook his head. "At first the cooking seemed silly, but after a while, I realized I loved what I was doing. My mornings are magic."

His moments, I thought.

I studied the man sitting next to me—my first love. Dad.

I turned my hands to hold his and stared into his eyes.

Back when I'd been four or five, I'd vowed to marry him someday, not fully grasping the whole rules-of-marriage thing. For me, there had been no one who could measure up to my dad.

"Good food fast." I repeated.

Dad nodded, and then he breathed out a sigh. "I should have told your mother what I was doing."

"You think?"

He smiled and unwrapped the sandwich.

"Did you make this?" I asked.

Another nod.

"How do you feel about cooking dinner from now on?"

And then we laughed, sitting together to share one of the best sandwiches I'd ever eaten.

When we were finished, I balanced my camera on the Beast's fender and used the timer setting to take a picture of Dad and me. Then I made another entry in my notebook.

Dad and me. Good food fast.

Perhaps everyone walked around with an unfulfilled dream inside them. Truth was, I was proud of Dad for acting on his when the opportunity presented itself.

Was he wrong in hiding his new job from Mom? Yes. But the fact he'd finally gone after what he wanted made him an even bigger hero in my eyes than he'd been all those years ago when I'd thought him the most wonderful man alive.

I wasn't looking forward to telling Jessica the truth about Johnny Testa's new cook, but then my mind hit on something else that I couldn't wait to tell her.

I thought about Dad's words. *Everyone's in a hurry.*

But were they? Really?

Maybe it didn't matter if Johnny's Test Kitchen served good food fast, because maybe Jessica's Paris Café served something Johnny's Test Kitchen never could.

∽

"Good food slow," I called out as I barreled through the café's front door.

Jessica spotted me and set a steaming mug of coffee at my favorite seat at the counter.

"Screw good food fast," I said, a bit too loudly, based on the frowns of her customers.

Jessica looked down at the counter to hide her laugh. "I think that whole *edgy* thing's coming together for you just fine."

I waved a hand dismissively as I slid onto the stool and set my camera on the spotless countertop. I jerked my thumb toward Johnny Testa's restaurant across the street. "He might have good food fast, but you've got what matters. You said it yourself. Good food. *Slow.*" I leaned forward. "Years of special moments."

"Special moments?" Jessica's squinted.

I nodded.

She took a backward step and frowned, visibly mulling over what I'd said. "Based on the way customers are flocking to him, they don't care about special moments." Her forehead wrinkled. "I need to do something drastic."

I took a long swallow of coffee before I pressed my palms to the counter and leaned forward. "Maybe this town's big enough for two restaurants. Maybe you need to keep things exactly as they are."

I twisted on the stool, craning my neck to study the other patrons. One of my mother's garden club buddies sat talking and laughing with her three grandchildren. From where I sat, it looked as though they were about halfway through their grilled cheese sandwiches and vanilla milk shakes.

I grabbed my camera and slid off my stool.

"What are you doing?" Jessica asked.

I pretended I didn't hear her. I popped off the lens cap and chose an automatic setting as I approached the booth. "Afternoon, Mrs. Jackson." I tipped my hat. "Rory, Matt, Josh. Mind if I take your picture?"

Sue Jackson's smile warmed. "I suppose not."

"Cheese!" Josh Jackson, the youngest of the three, struck a dramatic pose, arms flexed in a familiar little-boy show of strength.

Sue laughed. "I guess that's a yes. Snap away."

As I clicked off several shots, the small group's laughter grew. The children mugged for the camera, hugging one another, making faces, hamming it up as if they'd never posed for a photograph before.

When they changed sides of the booth to wrap their arms around their grandmother's neck, I knew I had my *moment* shot.

I pointed to the wall beside the counter where a framed print of the Paris Bridge now hung. "The next time you come in, you'll be able to see your picture. Matter of fact, you'll be the first on Jessica's new photo wall."

Whether she knew it or not, I thought.

Then I glanced over to where Jessica stood. Her features had brightened, and she smiled as she watched the small group beside me.

The Jackson grandchildren were still chattering excitedly as I made my way back to the counter and my mug of coffee. "Good food slow," I said as I sat down.

Jessica was still staring at the Jackson family, and if I wasn't mistaken, her eyes held a spark of interest.

It wasn't the oh-my-goodness-you're-a-genius-Abby response I might have hoped for. But I'd take what I could get.

CHAPTER TWENTY-TWO

Frankie sat with Mick's mother on the front porch of the O'Malley house later that afternoon. I spotted them as I pulled the Beast into our driveway and shifted the car into park.

The freshly painted steps had dried, as if infused with new life. The contrast between the restored risers and Detta O'Malley's frail frame made my heart ache.

No matter how many coats of paint Mick used, he'd never be able to stop the slow march of his mother's dementia; nor would he be able to erase the years he'd been gone.

As I walked across the lush spring grass of my parents' front lawn, Mrs. O'Malley wrung her hands. Frankie leaned close to the older woman, talking softly and regarding her with such palpable concern, the sight momentarily stole my breath.

"What's wrong?" I asked, keeping my voice low.

Detta shook her head and sighed. Frankie looked up at me and mouthed two words. *Trash day.*

I turned, shifting my gaze from the pair on the steps to the expanse of Third Avenue. Trash and recycling bins lined the curb just as they had the day I'd first found Detta wandering over on Bridge Street.

"Mick's afraid she'll walk off."

I sat down on the other side of Detta, gently placing my hand on her knee.

"Where is he?" I asked.

"At a meeting in town," Frankie said. "He asked me to sit with her. She's having a tough day."

I thought about how happy ripping up the garden had made Mrs. O'Malley, how being in control for just that little while had brought back the light in her eyes.

Couldn't we do the same for her now?

"Can't we walk with her?" I asked.

Frankie shook her head. "Mick said there's bad weather coming. He wants her to stay put."

I looked up. The sky above the trees to the east remained clear and blue, but a definite darkness hung to the west, most likely the sign of an incoming spring storm.

"What about a ride?" I asked, determined to give Mrs. O'Malley another moment.

Frankie pressed her lips into a thin line and frowned. "Mick said to stay put."

Another person might have called Mick to ask permission, but I didn't want to lose a minute in my race against the darkening sky.

I made an executive decision instead. The Halladay Cab Company was taking Detta O'Malley on a search for dead plants.

"Detta"—I took her hand as I spoke—"would you like to go for a ride?"

Frankie's eyes widened, and I shot her a reassuring smile. "This is on me," I said. "If he gets angry, I'll make sure he knows you had nothing to do with this."

A few moments later, we were all settled inside the cab and on our way.

"Such a lovely car," Detta said, her voice hoarse, as if she hadn't spoken yet today.

Her eyes lit as if she'd never seen the car before, even though the memory of her singing along to the Mamas and the Papas would be forever imprinted on my mind.

"This is our dad's cab." I met her gaze in the rearview mirror, ignoring the sadness that edged into my heart. "He calls her Bessie."

"Bessie," she said, running her hand across the leather seat, repeating the name softly, over and over again. "Bessie…Bessie… Bessie."

I drove first along Stone Lane then turned onto Bridge, slowing the Beast to a crawl as Mrs. O'Malley studied the trash cans lining the curb in front of the shops and businesses that wove the fabric of Paris's personality.

The cobblestone sidewalks were empty, a sure sign that both residents and tourists realized a downpour was imminent.

Mrs. O'Malley, Frankie, and I continued our search, undaunted by a chance of rain.

I turned from Bridge to Front, and from Front to First. At the end of each unsuccessful block, we'd release a collective sigh and move on.

I'd been listening to the Mamas and the Papas the last time I'd been in the Beast and powered on the CD player. I smiled as soft harmonies reverberated inside the cab, pushing away some of the anxiousness that had built with each unsuccessful block.

Detta sang along with the music, joy palpable in her smooth voice. Frankie leaned close to Detta, holding her hand and swaying to the music. Yet, even though they sang, Detta's focus remained unchanged, her attention held steadfastly by the clusters of trash bins and bags awaiting tomorrow's collection.

The song ended and we fell silent. I pulled to a stop at the end of First Street, realizing I'd grossly overestimated the possibility of finding a plant for Detta.

"Can we go where people die, dear?" Mrs. O'Malley's question surprised me with the force and lucidity of her words.

"The cemetery, Mrs. O'Malley?" I asked.

I turned to face the backseat. Frankie frowned, apparently as confused by the question as I was. Detta's features brightened momentarily before they visibly tensed as she tried to answer my question.

"I don't know," she said, all traces of vibrancy gone from her voice. Tears welled in her eyes.

"They have flowers at the cemetery." Frankie spoke softly, patting Detta's hand. "Do you want to go there?"

Detta shook her head and began to rock—forward and back, forward and back. The sky darkened as storm clouds churned and thickened above us. The first fat drops of rain hit the windshield, and Detta pulled at her seat belt, suddenly twisting against the strap, slapping at Frankie's hands.

Frankie did her best to hold Detta steady, but Mick's mother fought back with a strength that took me completely by surprise.

The next track of music began, but this time the voices and harmonies did nothing to soothe the loss of control inside the cab.

Detta connected with Frankie's cheek, her slap echoing the crack of thunder outside. I shifted Bessie into park and scrambled out of the car. As I opened the back passenger door, Detta clawed at my shirt, knocking my hat to the ground.

The skies had opened and rainwater streamed down upon us, coating the cab with a thick sheet of water, soaking me instantly through my layers of clothes.

"Are you all right?" I called out to my younger sister, hating the stunned hurt I spotted in her eyes.

She nodded, looking up at me helplessly. "Abby," she said, her one word conveying just how frightened she'd become.

"We're going home." I met her gaze and lied, working to hold my voice steady. "Everything's going to be all right."

I wrapped Detta in a hug, holding her arms against her sides as I spoke gently, calmly, keeping my lips close to her ear so she could hear me above the storm. "We're going home. Everything's going to be all right," I repeated.

Detta stilled momentarily, but then her crying intensified. She no longer thrashed against the seat belt, but sat calmly in my arms, tears trailing down her cheeks.

"I want to go where people die," she cried.

My heart pounded in my chest.

What did she mean? Even more important, what had I done?

I'd thought I could make her happy with a cab ride and a search for plants, but instead she was scared and crying, wanting only to go where people died.

Frankie had been right. We should have stayed put.

Detta raised her hand, pointing out the front window of the cab.

Rainwater streamed around me now, and a fresh crack of thunder left me more rattled than I'd been a moment earlier, which was difficult to imagine.

I gave Detta a quick squeeze, straightened fully into the storm, and slammed the car door shut. I plucked Dad's fedora from the puddle at my feet before I looked to where Detta had pointed.

I'd been expecting to see a building or a sign or something to help me figure out where she wanted to go. Instead, I saw Mick.

Rain sheeted off his windbreaker, and anger came off him in waves as he headed toward us from Artisan Alley.

I wanted nothing more than to go back to the moment I'd decided I knew what would be best for his mother.

"I'm sorry," I said, my voice barely audible above the torrential downpour.

He slowed his approach, as if knowing he wouldn't be able to contain his anger if he moved more quickly. His features twisted, and for a fleeting moment I looked into the face of his father.

Something flipped deep inside my belly, and I moved to close the space between us.

"I was wrong, Mick. Please don't blame Frankie. She told me to stay put. She listened to you. I didn't." I was babbling and I didn't care.

Perhaps the faster I talked, the more quickly his anger would dissipate. Perhaps his features would relax and we'd all go home. Perhaps this moment would be lost, forgotten, forgiven.

Yet Mick's features didn't relax. Instead, he stood in the pouring rain, waiting patiently until I was done trying to justify going against his wishes.

"I know she loves looking for plants," I continued. "I never stopped to think the storm would scare her. You know I'd never do anything to upset your mother. I'm sorry. I just didn't think."

I paused to take a breath and Mick spoke. I expected a raised voice. I expected a lecture. But in true Mick fashion, I got only a few, carefully chosen words, uttered in a calm, yet obviously angry tone.

"There are some things you just can't fix, Abby. This is one of them."

He walked past me to open the rear passenger door of the cab. He leaned in, kissed his mother's cheek, and checked her seat belt. Then he shut the door, opened the front passenger door, and climbed in, leaving me standing in the rain holding my hat.

I shook myself out of my trance and scrambled back to the driver's side.

"Home?" I asked as I climbed in. Mick nodded, and I snapped off the music and shifted Bessie into drive.

I did not look at or speak to Mick after that.

I was pretty sure he preferred things that way.

Detta's soft voice rose from the backseat. "I want to go where people die."

I turned slightly toward Mick.

"The funeral home," he said without waiting for my question. A muscle worked along his jaw.

The funeral home.

I mentally berated myself. How could I have not figured that out?

I followed Artisan to Race to Arch, heading for Maxwell's Mortuary, the closer of the two funeral homes in Paris.

As I slowed along the long expanse of curb that edged the mortuary's landscaped gardens, Detta squeaked with excitement from the backseat.

"Stay put, Mom," Mick said. "I'll get it for you."

Stay put.

The rain had slowed to a steady drizzle, and the skies had brightened. Mick climbed from the cab and plucked a nearly dead peace lily from beside a single trash can in front of the funeral home.

He carefully lifted the pot, protecting the plant's withered leaves as he hoisted the container into the crook of his arm.

Then he looked toward the cab and smiled.

I mentally withdrew my thought about his fresh coat of paint not making up for the years he'd been gone. Whether or not Mick had been gone from Paris wasn't what mattered. What mattered was that Mick was here now.

He settled the plant into Detta's arms and gave her a quick kiss on the cheek. "She's a beauty, Mom."

I turned the music back on as we headed home, not only to please Detta but also to drown out the tense silence that hovered between me and Mick in the front seat of the cab.

Detta's voice rose in song, clear and light. She cradled the peace lily as if holding a favorite pet, and I realized I'd been very wrong to think I understood the complexity of her condition.

I couldn't undo the moments of panic she'd felt during the height of the storm, but I could hope that somehow her brain would hold on to the joy she felt at that moment, cradling a single, bedraggled peace lily rescued by her loving son.

Back at the house, Frankie walked Detta inside, promising to take the lily out to the greenhouse after a little while.

"You don't know what you're dealing with," Mick said as I turned to climb back into the cab.

He was right. I had no idea of what I was dealing with. "I'm sorry."

Mick's eyes widened with disbelief. "Sorry? What if she'd gotten lost or hurt today, Abby? Did you think about that? There's more to keeping her safe and happy than ripping up a garden and petting a dog." He waved his hands, his anger palpable, borderline frightening in intensity.

"I wanted her to stay put," he said. "She should have stayed put."

"But she was okay until the storm started." I reached for him, but he quickly stepped out of range. "I never meant to upset her."

Mick ran a hand through his hair and shut his eyes momentarily, as if trying to maintain control. "You're not hearing what I'm saying."

"I'm hearing you just fine."

"Are you?" When his eyes met mine again, they flashed with frustration, a rare show of the emotions he typically kept so closely guarded. He leaned toward me, so close I held my breath.

He was right, and I knew it. And yet I couldn't bring myself to do anything but defend my actions—my actions, which had been careless.

Mick straightened, turned, and walked away.

I still said nothing.

Instead I stood on his front lawn, humbled and duly chastised, standing motionless in his wake.

Later that night, I sneaked a peek into Frankie's room. I had expected her to be awake, but instead found her room dark, her sleeping form nothing more than a lump beneath her covers.

Beside her head sat a black-and-white stuffed dog, a present from Don Michaels.

The dark and dreary magazine clippings and artwork that had once graced the expanse of bulletin board above Frankie's desk were gone. They'd been replaced with a variety of snapshots from Don and Riley's first visit.

I smiled. While the dog had been trained to touch the hearts of the patients he visited, he'd touched Frankie's heart in ways I could have never imagined or hoped for.

She'd announced her intention to train therapy dogs, which presented one minor problem. Years ago, my mother had handed down a no-pet rule, which still stood.

While I thought Frankie might be able to sway our dad, I wasn't sure about Mom. Yet Mom had sacrificed her garden for

Detta. Perhaps she would sacrifice her clean floors to let Frankie bring home a new dog.

"I'm not asleep," she mumbled. "You can stop snooping."

I sat on the edge of her bed, and she shifted to give me more room. "How's your cheek?" I asked.

After our excursion, Frankie had held a bag of frozen peas to her face for twenty minutes. And while she'd complained the entire time, the rest of the family knew we'd been spared from the tuna-and-pea casserole Mom had been planning for dinner.

Frankie gingerly rubbed her cheekbone. "It's not bad. She didn't mean to hurt me."

"I know." I brushed a lock of dark hair from her forehead, and she let me. "I'm sorry I didn't listen to you today. I was wrong."

Frankie pushed up on one elbow. "Wow. Should I record that?"

I stood and kissed the top of her head. "Nope. I'm just sorry I put you and Detta in that position."

"Have you apologized to Mick?"

"Not exactly." I straightened her covers before I turned for the door. "But I will."

That night, for the first time in days, I picked up the phone and dialed Fred's number. Maybe I hoped he'd listen to my message and tell me what I'd done was all right. Maybe I hoped he'd say he understood that I hadn't meant to harm Detta when I'd set out in the cab.

But I didn't need Fred to tell me. I didn't need anyone to tell me.

The truth was I'd been wrong. I'd been so caught up in the high of the moments I'd shared with Dad, Jessica, and Sue Jackson and her grandchildren that I'd thought I could fix Mrs. O'Malley with a new moment of her own.

I wanted to tell Fred how much the past few weeks had changed me. I wanted to see if he'd experienced something similar. After all, I did care about the man. I'd been about to marry him, for crying out loud.

I listened to Fred's outgoing message, pressed the end key, and powered down my phone.

I didn't need to share my day with Fred. I didn't want to share my day with Fred.

Perhaps today's moments weren't all perfect, but they were mine.

And at least for now, I wanted to keep them that way.

CHAPTER TWENTY-THREE

I spent the next few days working out new routes for the Beast, taking pictures, and falling in love with Paris. Perhaps I was still in denial about just how thoroughly all my former plans had fallen apart, but the truth was I felt happier than I had in years.

At Destiny's request, I'd stayed away from my house, letting her and Rock work their magic. Images of the gaping holes in the floors and walls remained crystal clear in my mind, but I trusted Destiny to make the house a home again.

We'd been fortunate enough to find the lumber we needed at the salvage yard Jessica had suggested. My next worry was how to afford the expense of the other materials. Destiny hadn't notified me that she needed them yet, but at the rate she and Rock were working, it wouldn't be too long.

Mick and I had managed to avoid each other since the day I'd taken his mother out into the storm. Frankie continued to rush home from school to sit beside Detta, yet she'd also begun training with Don. With my parents' approval, Frankie and I had accompanied Don and Riley on a few of their therapy visits.

On Wednesday afternoon, we visited the nursing home in the next town over.

I'd worried that Frankie might be frightened by the sounds and smells of the facility, but instead she'd come to life, taking instruction from Don, handling Riley like a pro, and playing guitar for the home's residents.

"You should have seen Riley," Frankie said, her features coming to life as she replayed the details of our visit during dinner that night.

"The residents were sitting in a big circle in the activity room and Riley moved from one to the other, wiggling in for a neck scratch." She laughed and pointed at me. "Remember how he did that the first time he visited Detta?"

I nodded.

"You should see him," she said as Mom, Dad, Nan, and Missy listened attentively. "He's amazing."

Frankie paused to take a drink of water as if totally parched by her uncharacteristic chatter. "You should go with us one day, Mom...Dad..." She hesitated. "You'd understand why I want to do the same thing as Mr. Michaels. I want to work with therapy dogs."

She sank against the back of her chair and smiled, wrapping her arms around herself. "Someday I want a dog just like Riley."

Over the past few years, I'd watched Frankie's expression and presence shift slowly from one of prepubescent wonder to one of pubescent isolation. Yet tonight, I found myself carried away from my own thoughts and questions of life by the excitement she conveyed for her work with Riley and Don.

It seemed I wasn't the only one who'd found my passion during the past few weeks. Frankie had found a passion of her own, and I couldn't be prouder.

Mom's eyes widened, and I realized she'd shifted from enjoying Frankie's chatter to imagining life with a dog.

"I say go for it," I said, drawing a sharp look from my mother. "Dreams are for chasing."

"Dreams *are* for chasing," Mom repeated. "But you have to be realistic. I'm not sure now's a good time for a dog."

The light in Frankie's eyes slipped, and my father's expression shifted from entertained to thoughtful. I wondered if he'd realized the same thing I had about Frankie's passion.

"I have to agree with Abby," he said. "Maybe now's a great time for a dog."

"Buddy?" Mom went a little pale.

"We should let her chase her dream, Madeline," Dad said with a nervous laugh. "We should all chase our dreams."

Mom's eyes narrowed, and my pulse quickened. Was he finally going to tell her how he spent his mornings?

Frankie, who typically bolted at the first sign of confrontation, sat and waited for Dad to say whatever it was he was about to say.

"I should have told you weeks ago"—Dad sat up a bit taller—"but I took a new job."

Mom said nothing. Her brows lifted marginally.

"I'm the morning cook at Johnny's Test Kitchen," Dad said, answering her unspoken question.

"This is where you go on the bike?" she asked.

Dad nodded.

Mom drew in a sharp breath and blinked, as if Dad's delay in telling her had affected her more than his actual news.

"Why *didn't* you tell me weeks ago?"

My father, who was no doubt accustomed to my mom questioning nothing, looked taken aback. Then his features softened, and I recognized the same open expression I'd witnessed the day he and I sat by the river.

"I'd like to tell you now."

Mom sat quietly for a moment and then she nodded. "I'd like that."

And then they sat and talked, my mother and father, as I hadn't heard them talk in years.

That night, I sat and wondered how many other teens did the sort of work Frankie had discovered. How many would want to, if they had the opportunity? How many seniors, like Don, spent their afternoons and weekends attending to the needs of others? How many stories were out there, like Frankie's and Don's, just waiting to be told?

Inspired, I put together a proposal for a series of feature articles for Max Campbell at the paper. With any luck at all, he'd give me a shot and help me launch my freelance career.

After I hit the send button, I sat back and stared at my wedding date, marked with a pink heart on the calendar. May eighteenth. Five weeks away.

I'd accepted the fact that—short of a miracle—there might not be a wedding.

I went through most days so focused on seeking out everyday moments and adding to the gallery of emotion and life inside the Beast, that I gave the impending date less and less thought.

My earlier conversation with Jessica ran through my mind, and I realized she was right. The more I let go of the life I'd planned, the more I began to love the life I had.

Funny how much a person's perspective could change over the course of a few weeks.

I headed for Jessica's café the next afternoon with four new pictures for the restaurant. While I wasn't sure the photo wall was doing anything to win back customers from Johnny's Test Kitchen, the project gave Jessica something tangible to focus on instead of staring out the window logging customers as they walked through her competitor's door.

I arrived just as the Clipper meeting swung into full action. Jessica had framed and hung the group photo I'd taken in the corner where they gathered each week, and I loved the way the picture captured the frenzied camaraderie the group shared every time they met.

"Argh, argh, argh," Mona Capshaw's voice sounded from the far corner.

I glanced at the meeting, surprised at the number of people gathered. "Wow, big meeting today."

Jessica shrugged. "Who doesn't love to save money?"

I twisted around to steal a look without looking like I was staring. Then I spotted Nan.

I gave her a quick wave, and she headed in my direction.

"How was your day, Macaroon?"

I pressed a kiss to her cheek. "Call me crazy, Nan, but I love driving the Beast."

She grinned and patted my hand. "Life has a funny way of working out."

Our gazes held, and in her eyes I saw the wisdom of a woman who had lived her entire life right here in small-town Paris. I knew how much she grieved for Grandpa, but she kept her eyes on the positive and never ceased to amaze me with her unfailing belief in me and my sisters.

"Thanks," I said softly. Then I drew in a breath and tipped my chin toward the Clippers. "I was about to head home, but I guess you want to stay for your meeting?"

She shook her head. "I was out for a walk and did a quick pop-in. Come on, you can drive me home."

A few moments later, Nan and I were settled inside the Beast, headed back toward Third Avenue.

"Any word from Fred?" she asked.

I shook my head, picturing the box of invitations now keeping the wedding binder company on the floor of my closet. I needed a resolution. Sure, I'd moved on with my life, but the uncertainty surrounding Fred's status hung over me like a cloud that couldn't decide whether to storm or float away.

"Maybe he's dead, dear," Nan said, with a bit too much delight in her voice.

"Nan!"

She snickered. "Sorry, but he deserves to be dead. And trust me, when your father gets a hold of him, he'll wish he was dead."

Disbelief washed through me. "I think Dad's happy Fred's gone."

"Maybe so, but no father is happy to see his daughter waffling around after getting her heart stomped on."

"What do you mean by *waffling*?"

"You've got no plans, Macaroon. Your house is under construction, sure, but your love life is in shambles, and you spend your days driving around in your dad's cab taking pictures."

I slowed the massive car to a stop at the corner. "Is this one of those reverse-psychology talks? Because I'm not sure it's working."

My grandmother laughed before she patted my shoulder. "I call 'em like I see 'em. You've had a plan since middle school." She paused to take a breath. "Yet here you are waffling."

Waffling.

At first I sulked. But then I smiled.

"I'm living in the now, Nan."

"The what?" she asked.

"The *now*."

"Is that what you call this?" She pointed to the array of photos that covered the front third of the cab's interior above the windshield.

"Yes." I pointed to the first photo I'd taken. Mona Capshaw. "See this? Mona's favorite moment that day was waking up."

Nan snickered.

I pointed to a second photograph. "Manny's nephew was spending the weekend when he lost his first tooth. Look how excited they both were."

"A moment?" Nan asked.

"A moment," I answered. "Life moments, Nan. Snapshots of the things and emotions that matter. The *now*. Not what was. Not what's supposed to be. Just what is.

"I was so busy planning for my future with Fred that I never stopped to appreciate"—I waved my hand across the line of photos—"this."

I expected Nan to launch into one of her legendary lectures, but instead she sat quietly, studying each photograph, her smile growing wide. My photography skills were improving, if I did say so myself.

I changed the subject just to be safe. "Keep an eye out for Mrs. O'Malley, please. It's trash day."

"Oh, she won't be out today, dear. She and Mick are coming over for an early supper."

CHAPTER TWENTY-FOUR

—— —— ——

"Can I help you get dinner ready?"

My mother looked up from tossing the salad, surprise mixing with pleasure in her expression. I wondered whether she was reacting to my question or my appearance.

I'd traded in Dad's plaid fedora for freshly washed and curled hair. I'd smoothed on a layer of lip gloss and had brushed a single coat of mascara on my eyelashes.

A small voice at the back of my brain questioned why I'd primped for the O'Malleys when I hadn't worried about my appearance for previous dinner guests.

Possible answers would be that I'd had a long morning and had wanted to freshen up. I wanted to make my mother smile. I wanted to prove I was moving forward with my life and self-esteem. There was also the possibility that I wanted to look good in front of Mick.

The little voice inside my head was having a field day with the question of why I cared about that.

I'd known Mick forever, and heaven knew he'd seen me at my worst. Perhaps I simply wanted to see his reaction to seeing me at my best.

"Why, Abby," my mom said. "You look lovely."

She set down the salad utensils and crossed to where I stood. She reached to tuck my hair behind my ears, and I let her. For once in my life I was ready to admit she'd been right all those years she'd told me to get my hair out of my face.

"Did you know we're having company for an early dinner?" she asked, one pale brow lifting with amusement. "More of a late lunch, actually."

"I might have heard something about that." I smoothed the front of the silky cream tunic I'd paired with a classic khaki skirt. "What do you think?"

Mom blinked, no doubt trying to contain her tears of joy at the sight of me wearing anything other than my recent uniform of jeans and a sweatshirt. "You look beautiful, sweetie."

She leaned in to kiss my cheek. "Beautiful inside and out," she whispered in my ear. "Don't ever let anyone make you doubt that."

Mick and Detta O'Malley arrived a few moments later, and we gathered around the dining room table, my family and our guests. Mom pulled open the blinds to allow the late-afternoon sun to shine into the house, and the play of light against the dishes and glasses was nothing short of dazzling.

No one argued. No one pouted. Frankie stayed through dessert *and* after-dinner conversation. Perhaps it was the company; perhaps it was the roast chicken that Mom let Dad prepare; perhaps it was the endless stream of corny jokes Missy told Mick in her efforts to win his heart, but dinner was as close to magical as a dinner could be, with one major exception.

Mick managed to avoid meeting my gaze for the entire meal. He hadn't laughed at anything I'd said, and he hadn't said a word about the fact I cleaned up well. Which I did.

Yet as dinner went on and Frankie hinted for the bazillionth time about wanting a dog of her own to train for therapy visits,

I realized Mick was bound and determined to ignore me. Plain and simple.

Mrs. O'Malley had begun to frown and worked her hands in her lap.

Mick's brows furrowed, and he pushed back his chair. "I hate to eat and run, but I think I'd better get Mom home. It's getting late."

"It's not even dark out yet," Missy whined.

Too young to understand the workings of dementia and the way the impending night often increased agitation, my youngest sister's only concern was in keeping Mick around as long as she could.

Mick kissed my mother's cheek and shook my father's hand. Then he gently hooked his mother's arm through his and walked her through the kitchen and out the back door, talking to her all the while, telling her how lovely she'd looked tonight at dinner.

Suddenly, even though he had succeeded in ignoring me through the entire meal, I couldn't think of a single person in the world I admired more.

A little while later, I stood at the kitchen sink, washing the dishes Frankie had cleared from the table. The last rays of sunlight sliced through the window above the sink, and my mother reached around me to hang a sun catcher.

The stained-glass piece, an intricate sun complete with rays of variegated length and width, combined color and design in a way I'd seen only in the windows of the Paris Gallery on Artisan Alley.

"Did you get that downtown?" I asked.

Mom shook her head and gave my shoulders a squeeze. "Mick brought it over as a thank-you gift for dinner."

"Oh." I tipped my head, studying the selection and play of color, so simple yet unexpected that it dared me to look away.

I thought of the beautiful stained glass hanging in the gallery's window the night I'd walked past, but I also flashed back on the items in Mick's basement.

His mother's, he'd said. But the suspicion gnawing at the base of my skull wondered whether or not Mick had given me the brush-off to hide the fact he'd learned to make art of his own.

"He must have gotten it at the gallery," I said, fishing for my answer. "They had several in their window the last time I walked past."

Mom laughed, the sound light and musical. "Mick doesn't buy them, dear. He makes them."

I envisioned the objects I'd spied on top of the table in the O'Malleys' basement—the leading, the glass, the green triangle I'd dropped and cracked—and I smiled.

Suddenly, I wanted to know what other secrets Mick O'Malley and his wall of silence held.

CHAPTER TWENTY-FIVE

—— —— ——

"Are you up there?"

I stared at the bottom rung of the tree house ladder and waited for Mick's answer, even though I knew he was there.

I'd heard him talking softly—on the phone, perhaps—when I'd first stepped outside to find him.

I knew he sat in the tree house many nights, using a baby monitor to listen in case his mother should call out from her sleep. Frankie had told me as much.

His words about asking for permission flickered through my brain, but I pushed right through them.

I climbed the ladder, the wood rough against the bottoms of my bare feet. I winced when I heard the unmistakable clink of beer bottle against beer bottle.

My head cleared the top step and our gazes met. Worry flowed through me momentarily. Had he been drinking? Was he drunk? Had coming here been a mistake?

Then I realized he was pushing around full bottles of beer, much as he'd done the first night we sat up here and talked. This time, however, not one bottle top had been removed.

"May I?" I asked, pointing to the interior of the structure.

Mick nodded. "It's a bit late to be asking permission now."

I settled a few feet away from him, utilizing the limited space the tree house had to offer.

"I never apologized for last week," I said.

But Mick only held up a hand to stop me. "Not tonight." He shook his head, his features slack, traces of defeat dancing in his eyes.

Alarm washed through me. "What's wrong? Is it your mom?"

"No." He hung his head. "She's as good as can be expected."

"You look like your dog died," I said.

"He did die." Mick's sudden grin wiped away much of my worry.

"Twenty years ago." I pointed to the bottles. "You sure you didn't drink some and put the tops back on?"

Mick's expression grew sad. "Too dangerous."

I narrowed my eyes, concerned, wondering if the call I'd overheard had anything to do with his shift in mood. "I heard you talking," I said, hating the note of hesitation heavy in my words.

"And yet you climbed right up that ladder." Mick ran a hand through his hair and squeezed his eyes so tightly shut crow's-feet appeared at their sides.

"Sorry." I spoke in little more than a whisper.

Mick drew in a slow, deep breath, as if undecided about engaging me in conversation. When he finally spoke, his answer deepened my confusion.

"Today is her birthday," he said.

I frowned. "I thought your mother's birthday was in the fall?"

Mick shook his head. "Not my mother."

"Oh." I straightened and sat back. "Your wife?"

But again he looked down, shaking his head.

"Who then?"

Mick looked down at his hand, and I realized he'd been palming something. He handed me the object—a photograph. Tattered and faded.

In the captured image, a toddler looked up at the camera, laughing, eyes bright, smile wide, two new white teeth gleaming from behind her bottom lip.

My heartbeat quickened. Was it possible? Was this—?

"Is this your daughter?" I asked, doing my best to brace myself for Mick's answer.

He nodded and rubbed his forehead, keeping his eyes shut and his brows furrowed. "This is Lily."

I refocused on the girl's image. Matching dimples. Identical eyes. Soft brown hair. "She's beautiful."

For a moment, the photograph slipped between my fingers, my surprise weakening my grip. But then I caught myself and the snapshot.

I handed the image back to Mick, who looked from my startled expression to the happy smile of his child.

"Was she with her mother...?" My voice trailed off, and I found myself unable to finish the question.

Mick shook his head. "She was home asleep in her crib when Mary drove into the tree."

The cold edge of his words sent a chill through my veins. While he might have once grieved for his wife, he'd apparently moved on to anger.

"Where is she?" I asked.

Mick uncapped the first bottle and poured beer over the side of the tree house. The amber liquid splashed against the lawn below, spattering against the base of the tree.

"I left her with her grandparents," Mick said flatly, without a trace of life in his voice.

"Mary's parents?"

He nodded. "They'd raised children." He popped another cap. "I hadn't."

I drew in a slow breath and released it, wanting to take my time before I spoke. There was so much I wanted to say, so much I wanted to argue, yet this was Mick.

He'd lived through thirteen years of which I had no first-person experience. I couldn't begin to frame what he was telling me against the context of his life.

I did know Mick, though. Or at least, I thought I did. Based on his interactions with his mother—and with me—he hadn't changed much from the Mick I'd known back in high school—the Mick who would do whatever it took to protect someone he loved.

I swallowed down my hesitation. "No one knows how to be a parent the first time."

He lifted his chin and glared at me. Hard. "I realize that."

"Did they ask for her?"

Several long seconds beat between us as his eyes locked on mine. He shook his head. "Worse. They expected her. They knew I'd be a lousy father."

Nerves simmered in the pit of my belly. Much as I wanted to talk to Mick, his anger boiled just below the surface of his control.

"Would you be a lousy father?" I asked.

He nodded. "Absolutely."

But I wasn't so sure. "Why would you say that?"

I'd seen him with Frankie and Missy and knew he was being unfair to himself, but I wasn't ready to push him. Not yet.

Mick stood up inside the tree house and paced. Not an easy feat. "Look at my role model."

I rubbed my face, fatigue and emotion getting the best of me. "Your mother has always been the kindest woman in this town. She's a wonderful mother. You could have brought Lily here."

Mick shook his head again, this time allowing himself a soft smile. "I wasn't talking about my mother."

Now I scrambled to my feet. "Your father? He isn't the one who shaped you, and you know—"

Mick held his hands up in the air, and I fell silent.

"I'm Ed O'Malley's son and the boy who burned down the Paris Oak. They might as well have put my name on the damn rock. I wasn't bringing my daughter back here."

The force of his words hit me like a freight train. The guilt that had swirled inside me for years, exploded. What had I done?

His gaze locked on mine. I'd never seen anyone look so angry or heartbroken in all my life.

I forced myself to stay on the topic at hand.

"Were you talking to Lily earlier?" I asked.

He nodded. "I tell her a bedtime story every night."

"When did you see her last?"

"A few days before I left to come back east."

A few days before I left.

I thought about Mick's words and realized that was how I'd remembered him for the past thirteen years.

Leaving.

One day he was here. The next he was gone.

Surely he wouldn't want his daughter growing up to think of him the same way.

He cupped the photo in his palm, staring down at the image of Lily, and the sight lodged in my brain.

"Did you see her?"

Mick nodded. "Every weekend."

Understanding clicked deep inside me.

It wasn't that Mick hadn't loved his daughter enough to raise her. He hadn't thought himself capable of raising her.

Sadness welled up inside me. "But you love her?" I asked.

His focus snapped so sharply to mine, I gasped.

Love and longing shone in Mick's eyes, doubt and remorse playing clearly across his features.

Could he have stayed? Should he have stayed?

Would he go back?

The thought of Mick leaving again pulled at me like a weight dragging me down from the emotional high I'd felt during dinner.

Mick had a daughter.

I said the words over and over in my mind, trying to add that piece of his life to the mental image I carried.

Mick had a daughter—a daughter he obviously loved and missed.

At some point, life—and Lily—would carry Mick O'Malley away from Paris again.

Then I thought of Detta, the sole reason for Mick's return to the town he'd once fled. "Does your mother remember her?"

He shook his head. "I flew her out west once, just after Lily was born. I showed her where we lived and the business I'd built." He drew in a sharp breath. "None of that exists for her now."

"I'm sorry."

"When I found out she was sick, I sold my half of the business to my partner and promised Lily I'd call her every night. I haven't missed one yet."

"Sounds to me like you're a good father, Mick."

He shook his head. "Too late for that now."

Silence hung between us, and I found it difficult to breathe. I'd thought I'd be able to help somehow, but Mick had been right when he'd talked about the glass in the basement.

I couldn't fix everything.

I couldn't fix this.

Suddenly overwhelmed by our conversation, I backed toward the ladder, needing to be anywhere but here, and wanting to leave Mick alone with his photograph and his thoughts.

"Abby?" he called out.

I froze, one hand on the top rung, the other two rungs below.

"Do you love him?" he asked.

The shift in conversation took me so utterly by surprise that a nervous laugh escaped me. "I don't know," I answered honestly.

Then I realized there was a question I'd wanted to ask Mick ever since we reconnected. "Did you love her?"

"Mary?"

I gave a single, sharp nod.

Mick crossed to the ladder, kneeling down so that our faces were mere inches apart.

"I thought so once," he said. "But now I'm not sure I ever did."

Then he stared at me, as if memorizing every inch of my face.

"If you want to take my mom out again, you can," he added. "Apology accepted."

Then he straightened, turned away, and popped open another bottle.

He waited until I cleared the ladder and crossed the lawn before he dumped the bottle's contents.

I could still hear the splashing as I climbed the front steps to my parents' house, stepped inside, and shut the door.

That night, I climbed into the depths of the bedroom closet once more, this time searching for the yearbooks I'd packed away years earlier.

On a crisp October night of our senior year, my class had painted the brick wall behind the school, as tradition dictated we should. When we were finished, we posed as a group, youthful determination and carefree joy plastered across our faces.

Later that same night, Mick and I broke into the old Bainbridge Estate, wanting to explore the secret passageways and underground tunnels of the abandoned mansion.

Through the years, I'd convinced myself our adventure had been Mick's idea, but that was nothing more than me buying into the lie I'd let everyone believe.

I'd wanted to explore the underground tunnels that linked the estate to the family's former businesses—the old bank and the general store. Mick had gone with me because he didn't want me to get in trouble.

A bitter laugh slid across my lips. Fat lot of good that had done.

We'd climbed the Paris Oak after we'd tired of our exploration. I'd been stupid enough to light a candle. I still wondered how I could have done something so utterly asinine.

When Mick had reached to extinguish the flame, I'd kissed him.

I could still remember the feel of his lips on mine. I could imagine the weight of his hand pulling me against his chest. I could still summon up the mixture of awe and nerves and adolescent curiosity that had consumed me in that moment.

And then we'd realized the tree was on fire.

We'd jumped, escaping unscathed, but by the time we'd gotten the attention of the fire department, it had been too late.

The tree was destroyed.

They'd held us for two hours until our parents came to bail us out.

Mick had run away the next morning, not giving the school a chance to expel him. He'd vanished without saying good-bye, and in time, I'd actually managed to stop reliving that night.

At least, I'd managed until I'd seen him on my parents' roof.

The town had blamed Mick, and I'd let them. After all, it was easy to blame Ed O'Malley's son. In their eyes, I was a good girl. Always had been. Always would be.

Shame on me.

As I studied the photo now, I understood how wrong I'd been back then to let Mick take the blame for me. I also understood something I'd denied for the past thirteen years.

I'd been falling in love with Mick O'Malley.

Sure, I'd loved him as a friend ever since I first climbed up into his tree house, but years later, as we sat on the school football field posing for this group shot, the camera had captured my true emotions.

The heart of the shot, my mother had called it.

Here it was, for everyone to see.

While every other senior faced the camera, I stared at Mick. Even in my profile, the heart of the shot was evident. I'd been in love with Mick.

The admission hit me like a ton of bricks, rocking my already fragile state of mind.

I raced to my laptop and fired it up, tapping my fingers impatiently while the machine went through its start-up paces.

As soon as my wallpaper appeared, I stared at the engagement picture of Fred and me. Our smiles were the stiff we're-having-our-picture-taken smiles that everyone perfects at some point during adulthood.

I needed something more. I needed a better example.

I opened my picture folder and scanned thumbnails until I found a few candid shots of the two of us, pictures sent by friends and colleagues.

Even there, neither of us looked at the other as I'd looked at Mick back in high school. Sure, there was a big difference between grown-up love and high school love, but the photos showed nothing more than two people attending various fund-raising and corporate functions together.

The photos showed no laughter, no gazing into each other's eyes, no heart. They captured only two people living the life they'd planned as the rest of the world passed them by.

The moments with Fred weren't *moments* at all. They were poses—poses of the way we thought our life should be.

Fred and I had gone through the motions—in our photographs and our life. We'd followed the plan we'd made, seeing each other on weekends, attending functions that would advance our careers or our social standing.

We'd laughed politely at each other's jokes and stories. We'd coexisted in a relationship, but based on what?

The question sobered me.

Had I ever truly loved Fred?

Fred had fit my plan. He hadn't challenged me. He hadn't inspired me to sit back and touch my lips in remembrance of his kiss. He hadn't haunted my dreams.

He hadn't awakened my emotions in ways they hadn't been awakened in years.

Mick had done those things.

Not Fred.

I reached for my cell phone and dialed Fred's number. I listened for the millionth mind-numbing time to his outgoing message regarding space and silence, and then I left another message, this one far different than my earlier messages.

"I'm done waffling, Fred."

I glanced out my window, catching a glimpse of where the Beast sat out back, beneath her protective tarp. "I'm changing lanes. I'm done watching life go by. Maybe you're done watching life go by, too. Maybe that's why you went to France.

"But the point of this message is to say, I won't be leaving any other messages. I hope you're happy, and I hope you've found whatever it is you wanted to find." I hesitated, my parting words stuck in my throat momentarily before I pushed them resolutely, positively free.

"Good-bye, Fred."

The time had come to let go of the life I'd planned.

I was ready to live the life that had found me, here, back home in Paris.

CHAPTER TWENTY-SIX

Two days later, on a sunny April afternoon, Frankie, Detta, Nan, and I piled into the Beast and headed for the far side of town and the park that ran alongside the Delaware River.

As I pulled the cab into the parking area, I spotted Don and Riley sitting on a bright red bench, patiently waiting for our arrival.

"There they are," Frankie called out from the backseat.

Nan moved her hand from her lap to her throat, and her nervousness wasn't lost on me.

Much as she'd had an obvious effect on Don, the distinguished gentleman had left a mark of his own on my grandmother.

Nan smoothed the front of her windbreaker then tucked a strand of wavy white hair behind one ear.

I studied her, amusement welling inside me. She turned to say something and caught me staring. She blushed.

"Here we are." I tipped my head toward Don. "And there they are. Ready, ladies?"

"Stay put, Mrs. O'Malley," Frankie said as she scrambled toward her door. "I'll be right around for you."

By the time Frankie rounded the Beast's massive trunk, Don stood beside Detta's door, holding the door wide as he reached to steady her.

She linked arms with Frankie and Don as the trio set out across the lawn toward the picnic area.

Riley trotted obediently beside the three, and I realized again that my recent problems were merely bumps in the road of my life.

I held the door open for Nan, amused to see her frowning slightly at the fact that Don hadn't said more than a quick hello.

"You okay?" I asked, biting back a smile.

"Should have brought my scarf," Nan grouched. "Too windy out here."

"Such is life along the river." I shut the car door after she stepped clear and then I headed for the trunk. "Good thing I brought a kite. Perfect day for it."

She smiled then, her momentary funk visibly lifting. "I do love a kite."

"I know." I anchored a well-loaded picnic basket over one arm, tucked the kite against my side, and winked as I reached for Nan's hand.

For the next hour or so, our little group relaxed beside the river.

A spring breeze hoisted the kite high into the air, the simple rainbow-colored diamond glowing against the brightness of the afternoon sun.

Beds of impatiens rimmed the fieldstone wall along the Delaware's bank. Soon they'd swell and spread, sending a cascade of white, red, and pink along the edge of the park's green expanse. For now, however, they held the promise of the future, much like that afternoon held for me.

I took the case off my Minolta, set the aperture and depth of field, and began to snap shots, hitting the film-advance lever rapidly, smiling as I captured image after image, moment after moment.

Riley sat steadfastly beside Detta, unerring in his devotion and duty. Nan chatted cautiously with Don, and if I wasn't mistaken, there was an interest in her gaze that mirrored the attraction in Don's.

Frankie ran beneath the kite, laughing with an uninhibited joy of which I'd forgotten her capable.

Moments. Simple moments. Moments I might never have witnessed had I not lost my column and taken over Dad's cab, had I not met Don and Riley on that stormy afternoon.

Life was unpredictable.

As I took stock of that moment, the people, and the impacts they'd each had on my recent life, I realized it was in the letting go and allowing life's moments to happen that we truly lived.

That night, before dinner, Mom and I sat on the floor of her bedroom, building a scrapbook for Detta O'Malley.

She meticulously trimmed patterns and shapes out of pre-printed sheets, framing photos as she anchored them to the scrapbook's pages.

She worked with patience and precision, her enjoyment evident in her body language and slight smile. As if sensing my scrutiny, she glanced up at me and smiled, her eyes sparkling.

"You're beautiful, Mom."

I wasn't sure when I'd last spoken those words, or if I'd ever spoken them. I'm sure I'd uttered them back when I was Missy's age, a time in every daughter's life when she thought her mother was the most beautiful woman in the world.

But as we sat together, building a book of memories for our neighbor, my mother truly was the most beautiful woman in the world.

For all of her telling me how to dress, how to brush my hair, and how to find a replacement fiancé, she loved me. She loved me as perhaps no one else in my life ever would.

Here she sat, helping me put together a scrapbook in order to preserve the moments I'd so carefully gathered for Detta.

I thought of Mick and how devastated he must be to see his mother slipping away from him, to see her looking at him with confusion in her eyes when her mind failed her, when the images of their shared past escaped her.

Mom's eyes filled with tears and she blinked them away, but not before I saw flashes of the past—the look of love in my mother's gaze filled with images of first words, skinned knees, and school-dance photographs.

My heart hurt, thinking Mick's mother was losing those images. Mick's mother would never remember her granddaughter, Lily, and Lily would never know the woman Detta had been, or the woman she'd become.

"Did Mick tell you about Lily?" I asked.

Mom smiled. "I caught him staring at her picture one day when he was taking a break from working on the roof."

"And he talked about her?"

"A little." She tipped her head to one side, and a hint of gray appeared at her hairline. Slowly, but surely, Madeline Halladay was learning to relax.

"I want to help him," I said.

Mom leaned forward to place her hand on top of mine. "It's not your problem to fix. Just listen when he talks, Abby. That's what you used to do best."

"Did you give him any advice?" I asked.

My mother had always loved Mick like the son she'd never had. I remembered overhearing her crying during the days after he ran away. At the time, I hadn't understood how she could be so upset about a neighbor. Now, as an adult, I'd come to appreciate the depths of my mother's compassion.

"I told him to follow his heart." She refocused on the scrapbook page, pressing another photo into place before she sat back to admire her work. "The heart is an amazing thing, Abby."

I wondered if she was talking about Mick, or me, or both.

"What if his heart is too afraid to go after what he wants?" I asked.

She reached over again, this time giving my hand a firm squeeze. "Maybe his heart just needs time."

Just after dinner, I'd tucked the snapshot Nan had given me in my sweatshirt pocket. The long-ago image of my mother weighed as heavy as if it were made from lead instead of photo paper.

"What would you do if you could follow your heart, Mom?"

She sat back a fraction of an inch, as if no one had asked her that question in a very long time.

"What would *you* do?" she asked.

I shook my head. "I asked you first."

She stared at me blankly, and I realized she either had no idea of what to say or she didn't know where to start.

I pulled the photo from my pocket and handed it to her.

Mom studied her own image, so young, so carefree. She traced a finger across the photograph. Her slight, melancholy smile pulled at my insides.

"What did you want back then?" I asked.

She lifted her gaze to mine, tears shimmering along her lower lashes. "That was a long time ago, sweetheart."

I moved beside her and wrapped my arm around her waist. "So?"

"It doesn't matter what I wanted back then," she whispered. "I wouldn't change a thing."

I pulled her tighter against me. "What did you dream about? What did you want to be?"

She pointed to the old Minolta, hanging from her neck in the photo.

"A photographer?" I asked.

She nodded, wiping at her eyes. "I dreamed I'd be a *National Geographic* photojournalist, traveling the world, capturing images that might touch someone"—she lifted her hand to my heart—"here."

I blinked away my own tears, heartbroken to hear the pain of her lost dream still echoing inside her.

She touched her fingers to my chin lightly. "Now you're taking pictures and touching lives," she continued. "I couldn't be prouder."

I pressed a kiss to her cheek and pushed to my feet. "I'll be right back."

In my old bedroom, I plucked the Minolta from the bureau where it sat, then walked back to my parents' room. I knelt beside Mom and sat the camera in her hands.

She drew in a sharp, surprised breath. "Oh, I couldn't."

I nodded, as sure of what I was doing as I'd ever been of anything. "You can't go back here"—I tapped the old snapshot—"but you can start again.

"Your turn," I whispered. Then I wrapped my arms around her and held on tight.

CHAPTER TWENTY-SEVEN

——— —— ———

I should have known Nan was up to something when she agreed to brunch with Don. After all, she'd had fear in her eyes since the moment they'd met, although that fear had been joined by a spark of attraction on the day we'd gone for our picnic.

On that day, Nan's eyes had danced with curiosity and fascination before she'd caught herself and shuttered her emotions.

As my family waited for her to come downstairs for her first date in six years, I imagined she'd sport her emotional armor, but I never thought she'd cover herself in physical armor, as well.

"Mother, what are you wearing?" Mom asked.

Missy, who had recently seen several minutes of *West Side Story* on cable television before Mom realized she'd sneaked out of bed, danced past singing, "When you're a Jet, you're a Jet all the way."

Frankie, whose own wardrobe had morphed from all black to warm combinations of color and denim, nodded as she took in Nan's outfit. "You look cool."

Don had yet to arrive, yet there Nan stood, wearing my grandpa's favorite herringbone jacket, his tie that looked like piano keys, and his chocolate-brown fedora.

While I was in no position to criticize her choice of headwear, she'd either gone off the deep end, or she thought her appearance would send Don screaming.

Dad peeked his head out from the kitchen where he had two pies baking. "If they're giving out free meals if you come in costume, you're going to be one cheap date."

My mother shot him a death glare, then she fisted her hands on her hips. "Mother?"

Much to her credit, Nan ignored every one of our comments, holding her chin high. "I'd prefer to be called Gus from here on out."

A burst of laughter sounded from the kitchen, where Dad had retreated. My mother ran a hand through her hair, leaving the usually perfect strands in a layered mess.

"I will not call you Gus," she said, pointing to the stairs. "You march up there right now and put on something appropriate."

A flush rose in Nan's cheeks. "I may have changed my name and my manner of dress, but I am still your mother, young lady. You would be wise to remember that."

Mom took a backward step at the same moment the doorbell rang. "Buddy?" she called out to my father, her tone pleading with him to do something…anything.

"I'll get it," Frankie called out in a singsong voice so out of character I pinched myself to make sure I was awake.

Don Michaels stood at the door, Riley by his side. Riley sported a pale-blue bandana that perfectly matched the pale-blue blazer Don wore over a white Oxford-cloth shirt and a pair of chinos. Frankie opened the screen door and ushered Don and his dog inside. She slowed to press a kiss to Nan's cheek before she and Riley headed toward the back door for a visit with Detta.

Much to his credit, Don's visible admiration held steady when he saw Nan. Amusement danced in his eyes. "You look dashing," he said, holding out his arm. "Shall we?"

Nan narrowed her eyes. "You should know I've changed my name to Gus."

"Gus," Don said with a nod and a shrug, pointing to her jacket. "I wasn't sure where you'd like to go for brunch, but, if it's all right with you, I think the country club's a smart choice. We'll put their dress code to shame."

Dad had emerged from the kitchen, visibly holding back his laughter. "Have a great time, you two."

Nan crossed the foyer toward Don, who held the screen door open.

"Just a minute," I said, turning to Mom. "May I borrow the camera?"

She nodded, although displeasure still hovered in her expression.

I raced for the camera, returning a moment later with the lens cap off and the settings ready to go.

Nan and Don posed awkwardly at first, a classic please-get-this-over-with-quickly stance. But then something interesting started to happen. Don put his arm around Nan's shoulder, and she frowned.

"Did you hear the one about the Irishman and the stiff in the sports jacket?" he said, his teasing tone evident.

Nan smirked.

I snapped off the shot.

"Did you hear the one about the old man who wouldn't take no for an answer?" Nan asked in rebuttal.

Don laughed, his grin wide. Nan smiled. If I wasn't mistaken, she actually giggled.

I snapped off another shot.

And then they were on their way.

A few hours later, Nan returned. She still wore Grandpa's hat and tie, but she carried his jacket over her arm. An unmistakable light danced in her eyes, and a happy warmth built inside me at the thought of her and Don becoming something more than acquaintances.

"How was it?" I asked as she passed me on the stairs.

"Okay." She tipped her chin, doing her best to appear aloof, but then she smiled and gave my arm a conspiratorial squeeze. "*Very* okay."

After she disappeared into her bedroom, I retraced my steps to my own room. I pulled out my notebook and flipped to my log of moments, smiling as I made a new entry.

I knew Nan would always hold tight to the memories and photos of her life with my grandfather, but perhaps the pictures I'd taken might mark the beginning of a new set of moments she'd share with Don.

Even though I hadn't yet had the photos developed, I made my entry just the same, fairly certain the moment I'd witnessed would be exactly what the camera had captured.

So I wrote. *First date. Nan meets her match.*

I met Destiny at my yellow Victorian before we headed to the Pub for karaoke night.

She and Rock had been working nonstop to erase all signs of termite infestation, and I knew she was anxious to show me what they'd accomplished.

After seeing just how extensive the damage had been, I had no idea of what to expect. The sight that greeted me blew my mind.

"I'm speechless," I said.

Destiny laughed, pride shining in her gaze as she studied my reaction.

We stood in the doorway to the living room, where I could do nothing more than shake my head in amazement.

Where two weeks earlier there had been cutout walls and exposed studs, splintered floorboards, and baseboards reduced to termite-damaged pulp, there now stood restored and sanded floors, new baseboards, and unblemished walls.

"I went with the pine we found at the salvage yard," Destiny said as she stepped out ahead of me. "I wanted to keep things as authentic as I could."

I dropped to my knees and rubbed my palm across the smooth, flawless wood that had replaced the spot where gaping holes had loomed liked abscesses. My vision swam, and I blinked, sending a tear spilling over my lower lid.

The drop fell to the floor, a happy tear in the place where I'd previously felt nothing but overwhelming disbelief.

"How did you do this?" I lifted my gaze to Destiny's proud smile. "Have you slept in the past two weeks? And you haven't even given me a bill for some of these materials."

She waved off my concern and my gratitude. "We'll deal with that later."

I pushed to my feet and wrapped my arms around her, surprising her with both the move and the unspoken emotion.

I held tight as I spun her in a slow circle, taking in the freshly installed walls and the beautiful molding where before there had been only pulp and sawdust.

"I still have to finish the floors and reinstall your radiators," she said, laughter ringing through her words as she hugged me back. "Then you can pick your paint and trim colors."

I stopped spinning and released her from my grip. I stepped toward the wall and ran my fingertips down the smooth surface then along the expertly fitted trim. "It's amazing."

I stood motionless for a moment, overwhelmed by the changes that had taken place in my life. They had all started here. Just as Destiny had restored my house, cutting out the bad and lovingly fitting the new, my time without Fred had done the same for me.

Had it really been only a month since the termites had sent me scrambling back to my parents' house? Fred's month of silence was almost up as well. I shoved the thought away and focused on the house.

Destiny turned to point out a feature in the kitchen, but I grabbed for her elbow and held tight, turning her to face me.

"You. Are. Amazing." I grasped her arms and gave her a quick shake. "Amazing. I can never thank you enough."

Sudden moisture shimmered in Destiny's eyes. I had to admit, I'd never seen her tear up, not in twenty-five years of friendship. She cleared her throat and blinked. "Want to see the basement?"

I nodded, and after a tour of my newly restored ceiling joists and beams and my now structurally sound foundation and sill, we headed out into the Paris night to celebrate, two friends who'd known each other forever without really knowing each other at all.

Jerry had our beers waiting, and as I studied the crowd gathered for karaoke night, I did not see people my parents knew in the town where I'd grown up. I saw people *I* knew. I saw my friends and my neighbors in the town where I *lived*.

∽

Two beers later, Jerry called for singers, and I raised my hand for sign-up without hesitation.

The time had come to reclaim the things I loved.

The face of my phone illuminated where it sat atop the bar, and I leaned forward to read the display, my heart seizing in my chest as I read the words.

New text message. Fred.

"Shit."

"Abby Halladay," Jerry called out. "Come on down."

I waved off Jerry's request and dropped my arm to my lap.

"Abby?" Destiny's laughter morphed to concern. "You okay?"

I smoothed my finger across the screen to unlock my phone, then pressed View Now to read Fred's message, the first in four weeks.

Four weeks, I thought. The days seemed like so many more, and yet it seemed as though they'd passed in the blink of an eye.

Home by Sunday. Dinner at the café?

Surprise and doubt tangled inside me. He'd walked out a month ago and now he expected to waltz back in. I'd moved on. I'd started to build a new life.

I pressed the reply button, but Destiny slid my phone out from beneath my hand. "Make him wait."

She lifted my chin with her fingertips and stared into my eyes. "Sing," she said. "You wanted to sing. Don't let him take that away."

All I could do was shake my head. My knot of emotions overwhelmed me, and I hopped down from my stool.

How could one short text message begin to unravel the new me I'd worked so hard to achieve?

"I need some air."

"Abby!" Destiny called after me.

I was already halfway across the floor, headed past the stage.

Jerry called my name again as if he believed this time I'd follow through, take the microphone in my hand, and perform.

Instead, I pushed out into the darkness of Paris and walked.

With seven words, sent via text message, Fred had rocked my resolve to be happy with the life I'd found.

Yet it wasn't Fred's message that sent me reeling.

No.

What sent me reeling was the speed with which my self-doubt roared back to life, leaving me unsure of every decision I'd made.

CHAPTER TWENTY-EIGHT

___ ___ ___

I wandered the streets of Paris, trailing my fingers across the brightly colored shop doors and storefront windows. I walked past the cemetery and the library, wondering if Nan had been here tonight, or if she was finally ready to let go of her nightly chats with Grandpa.

I peered in the window of the Paris Café, squinting to see the wall of photos I'd shot and posted for Jessica and her customers.

I haunted the cobblestone sidewalks and alleyways, feeling as though I were living out one of my dreams, searching for something, yet not knowing what that something might possibly be.

A few hours earlier, I'd been secure in every decision I'd made since Fred left. But now...

Now I wasn't certain of anything at all.

What was wrong with me?

I headed back home in search of the one thing I'd thought I'd never look at again. My wedding binder.

I'd left the Beast back at the Pub. My father would no doubt kill me later for leaving her out, exposed to the damp night air that rolled in off the Delaware River.

Guilt flickered through me, but I slapped the sensation away.

The house was silent as I walked back inside, and I made my way to my room without making a sound, ditching the cab keys and Dad's fedora on the chair in the hall as I walked past.

Upstairs, in the bottom of the closet, I grasped the binder's vinyl cover. I tugged the monstrous object free and landed on the floor, legs spread-eagle, binder in my lap, the homemade cover laughing up at me, mocking me with its naive lettering.

Abby and Fred.

I'd designed the words on a desktop publishing program at work, spending more time choosing a font and border than I spent on most answers I gave to my "If You Can't Say Anything Nice" inquiries.

A month ago, the wedding and my column had been front and center in my world.

As I flipped through page after page of sheet-protected ideas and plans, I realized I'd stopped fighting for Fred and my engagement as soon as I'd gotten a better offer. Namely, a life driving a cab and taking pictures.

So, what did that say about me as a person? As a fiancée?

Sure, Fred had effectively locked me out of his life for the past month, but what if he'd had a really good reason? What if he couldn't wait to tell me about the things he'd seen and the things he'd done?

What if he was about to come home as renewed in his determination to live life as I'd become to live mine?

Didn't I at least owe a reply and some loving patience to the man I'd thought I'd loved?

I slid the fat binder off my lap and pulled my cell phone out of my pocket.

I reread Fred's text message.

Home by Sunday. Dinner at the café?

I read the words again. And again. And again.

I shoved down the angry voice that wanted to tell him to go to hell, and I embraced the tiny voice that told me to be nice and argued for giving the man a second chance.

Then I pressed the reply button and opened the phone's keyboard, typing quickly before I could change my mind.

This was the right thing to do. The grown-up thing to do. The responsible, we-had-a-plan-and-I-need-to-make-sure-I-haven't-made-a-mistake thing to do.

I kept my reply short and to the point.

See you then. Safe travels.

I hadn't professed my love. I hadn't told him I'd missed him. I'd merely communicated that I'd see him. I'd give him a chance to talk.

For now, that was all I could handle.

I woke at four o'clock in the morning, facedown in the binder, my nose wedged between cake selection and how to choreograph a first-dance production.

Bessie.

The image of the cab flashed across my mind like a neon billboard silently chastising me. *How could you do this? How could you leave me alone? Don't you love me anymore?*

I scrambled off my bed and raced for the downstairs hall, not taking time to step lightly around known creaks and groans. The keys and fedora sat on the credenza, not the chair where I'd tossed them. They'd been straightened and set precisely, just as my father used to do.

"She's okay." Dad's voice rang out from behind me as he followed me down the stairs, startling me so much I gasped and clutched my chest.

I turned to face him, the heat of shame rising up my neck. "I'm sorry, Dad, I—"

He shook his head and gave me the slight smile he always gave just before he said, "It's okay." Then he added, "Destiny called us on the house phone."

"She did?"

He shrugged. "I think she's turning into a softy."

I smiled.

His lips thinned and he clasped his hands on my shoulders, holding me steady. I began to tremble, an odd, quivering sensation that started deep inside me and built as it reached for my extremities.

"She wanted to see if you were all right."

"Did she tell you?" I wasn't sure if I was ready to see Fred, let alone tell my family about his impending return home.

"Only because she knew you were upset," Dad said. "You okay?"

I nodded, the move a bald-faced lie when all I felt was inner turmoil. "Where's Bessie?"

"Under her tent." He turned me toward the kitchen and looped his arm through mine. "Once I found you sleeping in your room, I headed to the Pub to pick her up."

"Sorry," I mumbled, feeling more like a three-year-old than a thirty-year-old.

"For what?" Dad pulled out a kitchen chair as he clicked on the overhead light. "For having a momentary lapse in judgment because that no-good Fred attempted a reentry into your life via text message like the chicken-livered louse he is?"

I couldn't help but laugh, my heart warming a bit at the depth of protectiveness in my dad's words. "How do you really feel?" I asked.

Dad moved to the counter and pulled out the griddle. Then he reached for his favorite mixing bowl and began to shift ingredients from the refrigerator to the counter, measuring by eye, mixing and blending.

He set the griddle on the stove and fired up the gas burner.

"Pancakes?" I asked.

"Pancakes," he answered.

Then I watched him cook, giving silent thanks for my dad and the realization that no matter how old you were, no one understood you or loved you like family.

CHAPTER TWENTY-NINE

I went through the motions the next day, driving fares to their destinations without engaging them in conversation, without asking about their days or about their favorite moments.

When I spotted Don and Riley standing on the corner of Bridge and Arch, I smiled, until I realized how utterly defeated Don looked.

"Tough day?" I asked as he opened the back door to climb inside.

Riley bounded into the car and leaned across the back of my seat to slurp my ear. I ruffled the white stripe that ran between his ears and over the top of his head. I couldn't help but wonder whether Frankie would still be sitting on the center hall steps, dressed in head-to-toe black, without this dog's help. Hell, without this man's help.

Don had taken Frankie under his wing, not only letting her ride along on therapy visits, but also introducing her to the folks he trained with.

She'd stated again that she wanted nothing for her birthday or Christmas—this year or any year. Nothing, that was, except for a dog of her own that she could train.

I was fairly certain the slide show I'd sensed flashing inside my mother's head included images of dog hair and muddy footprints. Though I also had a feeling Mom would eventually relent.

She'd begun taking the Minolta out on long walks around town. Once she started truly practicing her photography, she was bound to spend less time worrying about how perfect the house looked.

"Don?" I reached back and lightly touched the older man's arm. "Are you all right?"

He nodded. "Sorry," he said. "Mrs. Murphy's slipped into a coma. It won't be long now."

Melancholy touched my heart. The Widow Murphy had always seemed immortal to me as a child. Infallible. And yet, she wasn't.

None of us were.

"I'm sorry," I said. "Will you still visit?"

Riley gave a soft whine and set his head on Don's knee. "Good boy." Don wove his fingers through the fur at Riley's neck. "We'll visit until she leaves us," he answered. "She may not be awake, but she knows when Riley's there. I'm sure."

A tangle of emotion battled for space inside my heart. Sadness that Mrs. Murphy was nearing the end of her life. Happiness that she'd had the chance to know Don and Riley. Joy that I'd run into Don on that stormy day not too long ago, and now he'd become an ever more important part of my life, Frankie's life, and my grandmother's life—he and Nan had gone out on a handful of dates since their first.

"How goes it with Nan?" I asked, hoping a change in topic might ease Don's heartache.

Much to my surprise, he blushed.

"Sorry." I waved a hand as I turned back to drive Bessie. "Didn't mean to pry. I just meant, thanks for liking Nan. I mean, thanks for being such a great guy." I gave another wave as I pulled the car away from the curb. "Oh, never mind."

Don's laughter built from an amused chuckle to a full-out roar. "You're one in a million, Abby. How lucky am I that you gave me a ride that rainy afternoon."

Now I was the one blushing. "I was just thinking how lucky I was that you spotted the cab."

Silence beat between us for a few moments.

"Well," I said softly, "I'm glad you and Nan are enjoying each other's company."

Don nodded, looking out the window. While he didn't say a word, the slight upturn of his lips told me everything I needed to know. His was the face of a man who was falling in love.

"She's being a little stubborn about returning my calls this week. Something about being unfaithful to your grandpa." He winked at me in the rearview mirror. "You Halladay women…" His voice trailed off, but his smile remained firmly in place.

"We're trouble," I answered. "But I guarantee we're worth the effort."

Perhaps the no-secret-is-safe vibe of Paris had gotten to me. Perhaps I was more like my mother than I knew. Perhaps I just wanted Nan to be happy.

And so, sitting inside Dad's cab, I shared Nan's secret. Was I wrong to do so? Maybe. But maybe I was right.

Maybe, by giving away the secret to Nan's most-cherished daily moment, I'd be able to help her find a lifetime of new ones.

Later that afternoon, after I'd done a round-trip to Newark International and two smaller runs to Quaker Bridge Mall, I pulled Bessie to a stop just inside the gates of the Paris Cemetery. I left Dad's fedora on the front passenger seat and walked to Grandpa's grave.

I sank down onto the bench my family had installed years earlier, and rested my chin on my fists.

I thought about how many nights Nan had spent here, sipping tea in this very spot, bringing Grandpa up-to-date on her day and our lives. I thought about telling him about my month, but I figured he already knew…so to speak.

Sometimes I missed him so badly I ached inside. He'd been as loving and generous as anyone I'd ever met. I smiled. My mother's apple didn't fall far from that tree.

So today, instead of talking, I listened. The breeze rustled a nearby stand of cherry trees, and the Delaware washed past in the distance, a reminder that life was forever in motion, not waiting for us to make up our minds or shift our plans.

Life was a lot like driving Dad's cab. The trick to avoiding a fender bender was to react quickly and anticipate bad drivers. I thought about Fred and realized I hadn't done either very well lately.

His sudden departure had left me reeling, but I'd adapted. As a matter of fact, I liked the changes I'd made in my life during the past four weeks. I liked driving Bessie. I loved getting to know the residents of Paris. I was proud of my photo gallery inside the cab and at Jessica's. I even liked the Clippers, not that I'd ever admit that to anyone.

I felt stronger and more confident than I'd felt in years. So why had I let Fred's text message shake me to the core?

Part of me didn't want to face Fred. Part of me wanted to tell him to simply go away and stay away.

Yet an even bigger part of me knew that if I didn't face him and talk to him, I'd never really know how I felt about the man I had planned to marry.

New life plan or no new life plan, I couldn't move forward until I'd dealt with that part of my past.

My cell phone rang before I had time to answer my own question.

For a moment, I actually thought it might be Fred, but Max Campbell's voice took me completely by surprise.

Maybe he'd liked my new ideas. Maybe he'd decided to feature one of my articles.

"Listen, Henry's decided to retire. Obituaries and Celebrations is yours if you want them."

"Obituaries and Celebrations"? I tipped my head toward the sky and squinted at the stars. *Really?* I mouthed. But to Max, I said, "What about my other ideas?"

"Not edgy enough," he answered.

I wondered if he lived by that mantra, or if he saved the three-word phrase exclusively for me.

"Like Obituaries and Celebrations is?" Disbelief rang heavy in my tone.

"Not edgy," he agreed. "But most everyone gets married, promoted, or dies sooner or later."

His words still rang in my ears after I'd told him I'd think about his offer and hung up.

Most everyone gets married, promoted, or dies sooner or later.

Sure. But did I want to be the one to write about it?

Yes, a new gig meant I'd be back on payroll and collecting a steady—albeit small—paycheck, but did I want to sell out the dreams I'd newly embraced?

If Fred were involved in the decision, he'd be making a list of pros and cons as well as a potential earnings spreadsheet.

"I thought I'd find you here."

Mick's voice came out of nowhere, and if I hadn't seen his handsome face immediately, I probably would have written off his voice as a figment of my overactive imagination.

We hadn't seen each other since the infamous text message from Fred, but Mick had surely heard about it by now. This was Paris, after all.

He sat beside me on the bench and put his hand on my knee.

He said something, but my brain was too busy analyzing his hand on my knee to do anything even close to listening.

"Sorry?" I said, realizing I had no idea what he'd said.

"Are you keeping Nan's seat warm?" he said, apparently repeating what I'd missed.

I frowned. "You know about that?"

Mick grinned. "It's Paris. Everyone knows about that."

I smiled at the note of sympathy in his voice, as if he hated to be the one to tell me there were no secrets in a town this size. I'd learned that lesson in kindergarten, when I'd lost my first tooth over on the playground, and my mother had been notified and was waiting by the time I raced home.

"You're saying my detective skills aren't above average?" I asked, suddenly aware of how close we sat to each other.

"I'm sure they are." Mick took his hand from my knee and leaned forward, staring at the expanse of the cemetery.

I followed his gaze, taking in the headstones, the grave markers, the flowers, shrubs, and the ivy that had held its ground for hundreds of years.

Mick's family plot sat several yards away, and although I tried to imagine him stopping to pay his respects at the simple grave marker that marked the spot where Ed O'Malley's coffin had been buried, I couldn't.

"Where's your father?" I asked.

Mick pointed, even though he knew I knew exactly where the grave sat.

"Want me to give you some privacy?"

Mick laughed, the sound forced. "Hell, no. I'm not here for him. Do you know she never stopped buying him doughnuts?" he asked, his voice going thick. "Until she forgot."

Confusion swirled inside me. "Who?"

"Mom. That's when she got lost the first time." He hung his head. "At least, I think it was the first time."

I held tight to the arm of the bench, unnerved by the vulnerability in Mick's tone, my mom's words playing through my mind.

Listen to him when he talks.

"She'd gone to the bakery," Mick continued. "The old man loved glazed doughnuts. Plain glazed doughnuts." Mick ran a hand through his hair. "He was a drunk who made no time for us, and she still bought him his doughnuts even though he'd been dead for years."

I said nothing, not wanting to do or say anything that might shut down Mick's words.

"Your mother told me my mom wandered all the way to the bridge before Frankie spotted her and walked her home," he continued.

My mother had never told me a thing about Detta O'Malley's condition. She hadn't so much as hinted or gossiped about our neighbor's mental changes until I'd witnessed them for myself.

I'd once lumped my mother in with the rest of the Paris grapevine, but the past few weeks had taught me differently.

"Your mother took her to the doctor. Your father slept nights on her sofa until I got home. Your family was there when my mother had no one else."

I sat back, stunned by Mick's admission.

I'd had no idea of what had happened before Mick came home, but, at that moment, I couldn't have been prouder of my family.

We might have all grown apart there for a bit, but truth was, one thing had never changed. My family was one in a million.

I reached for his hand and he let me.

Mick stared at the ground between his boots. "Someday soon she won't remember me. I wasted all that time when I should have been here."

I tried to imagine how he felt, faced with the fact that the day would come in which his mother would no longer know him. The mere thought conjured such painful emotions I blinked back tears, my heart threatening to shatter.

Then it hit me.

"Some things run deeper than memory." I squeezed his hand in mine. "Like your mom's love."

He lifted his focus and our gazes met and held once more. "I'm sorry, Abby."

Sorry.

"Your mother understands," I said.

Mick shook his head. "I'm sorry I left without saying good-bye."

His simple sentence rocked me, erasing any trace of anger I'd held on to for the past dozen years.

Emotion tightened my throat. "I'm sorry, too," I whispered.

Mick frowned. "For what?"

"For letting everyone in Paris believe burning down the tree was your fault."

He smiled. "Didn't matter. You were the one headed to college. I was the son of the town drunk. Everyone expected me to be the one to screw up."

Frustration built inside me. "That's not true. Look at everything you've accomplished since then."

Mick pulled his hand free of mine and pushed to his feet. "I wouldn't have accomplished any of it if I'd stayed here." He gestured toward the gate. "Let's go."

I pressed a kiss to my fingertips and brushed them against the top of Grandpa's headstone before we stepped away.

Mick strode past his family plot without so much as a hesitant step or a sideways glance.

It felt right to have him beside me, strolling along as we'd done so many years ago.

"What are you going to do?" he asked after we'd climbed inside Bessie and were headed for home.

"About?"

He stretched, rolling his neck to the back, to the side, to the back again. "Your life."

"That, Mick O'Malley, is the million-dollar question."

"Seems to me you're happy now."

In my heart, I knew he was right, but I wasn't sure I was ready to make that admission. "What about you?" I asked.

"I'm happy here," he said.

He spoke the words quickly and assuredly but without conviction. A note of sadness tinged his tone, and I knew Lily must be ever present in his mind.

"Are you really?" I asked.

Mick said nothing.

I decided to push against the safe limits of our previous conversation. "Seems to me a big chunk of your happiness lives on the other side of the country."

Neither of us said another word during the remainder of the short ride home. After I pulled Bessie into her parking spot, safely beneath her tent, Mick climbed out.

Then he simply walked away.

CHAPTER THIRTY

— — —

That night, my mother did something she hadn't done in two weeks. She invited a bachelor to dinner.

Jack Maxwell, proprietor of Maxwell's Mortuary, sat sharing bruschetta with Dad as I walked into the dining room. I gave my eyes a quick rub in case I'd completely lost my mind or passed out or something.

Once upon a time, in the seventh grade, I'd had a short-lived crush on Jack. Surely my mother wasn't looking to reignite that flame now.

I found Mom in the kitchen, lovingly taking Dad's lasagna out of the oven.

I pointed back toward the dinner table. "Please tell me you're preplanning your funeral."

Mom screwed up her face and blinked. "Nope."

I leaned against the counter and dropped my voice low. "I thought we were done with the bachelor parade."

She shrugged. "Doesn't hurt to keep your options open." She carried the lasagna toward the dining room. "Grab the rolls from the oven, dear," she called out. "Your father made them from scratch."

I grabbed the rolls and followed, in no way done with our conversation. "Mom, you can't just walk out when someone's talking." I nodded at Jack. "Nice to see you, Jack. How's business?"

"Slow," he answered with a frown. Of course, I couldn't remember when I'd last seen Jack Maxwell without a frown. His brother had taken off years ago, leaving Jack with a business no one was entirely sure Jack wanted.

He studied the lasagna and his frown deepened. Amazing.

"Did you know the word *lasagna* comes from the name for the original pot, not the food itself?"

That was the other thing about Jack. He had an unfortunate habit of spouting off trivia whenever he got nervous.

"Fascinating," Nan said, giving Jack a kind smile.

My mom dished out generous servings of lasagna before we each filled our plates with rolls, salad, and mixed vegetables.

I pushed my food around on my plate, taking a forkful of steamed veggies before I set them back down, uneaten. "I can't believe you did this, Mom."

"It was nothing, really." She beamed. "Your father's teaching me a thing or two in the kitchen."

I blew out a sigh. She couldn't fool me. She knew exactly what I was talking about.

"I'm not talking about the food, and you know it."

My mother pushed to her feet and scowled, two moves so completely out of character everyone at the table froze, some while holding their forks in midair.

"Abigail Marie," she said. "I will not sit back and watch you pretend the last month never happened." She pointed her finger, her hand shaking. "I will not sit back and watch you question every decision you've made."

My father reached for her arm, but she brushed off his touch. Nan sat back and smiled, pride shining in her gaze.

Mom leaned forward, as if she and I were the only two people in the room. "Options, young lady. You have options. Don't you forget it."

She sank back into her chair and forked a mouthful of lasagna into her mouth as if nothing had happened. "Mm, I can hardly believe I made this." She smiled at my dad. "Thank you, honey."

The rest of us remained frozen. Shell-shocked.

Madeline Halladay did not have outbursts. Plain and simple.

"Did you know Garfield's favorite food is lasagna?" Jack asked.

"The president?" Dad asked.

Jack shook his head. "The cartoon character."

Frankie grabbed her plate, her fork, and her glass of milk. "I'm out of here," she said as she stood and pushed away from the table.

Dad set down his fork, narrowing his gaze on Frankie. "Francine Halladay. Sit back down."

Frankie hesitated, took one look at my father's face, and returned to her seat.

Mom looked down at her food to hide her smile. Missy took a sip of milk. Nan closed her eyes and drew in a deep breath. Jack shoveled lasagna into his mouth as if he hadn't eaten in a month.

I studied them—with the exception of Jack—and took stock of how far we'd all come in the past month. Every single one of us had changed, except Missy, who soldiered on happily as any smart five-year-old would.

"Options?" This time, I pushed to my feet. "We all have options."

I pointed to my dad. "You chose to chase your dream and cook for Johnny Testa, but you could be cooking for Jessica. She's been my friend my whole life, and my dad jumps sides to cook for the competition?"

Dad sat back in his chair, his features tensing with surprise at my outburst.

"And you." I pointed to my mom. "You have the most options of all." I paced away from the chair, crossed to the dining room window and back. "Missy starts school in the fall. Take the camera and chase *your* dream. Hang up the perfectly pressed aprons and the fashion magazine clothes and get your hands dirty."

I stopped and pivoted on my heel. "Remember how good it felt to let Mrs. O'Malley rip out your garden?"

Mom nodded slightly, but her eyes had gone huge.

"Give that same control to yourself. You deserve it, Mom.

"And you." I pointed at Nan. "Everyone knows you sit at Grandpa's grave every night. And guess what? None of them would think any less of you if you stopped. No one would think you're a bad person if you decided to have a life. Don Michaels adores you."

A slight flush colored her cheeks.

"He makes you happy, Nan," I continued. "Don't you think Grandpa would want that for you?

"Look at Frankie," I continued. "Her devotion to Mrs. O'Malley and her love of Don's dog have opened a whole new world for her. How many teenagers do you know who would choose working with therapy dogs over sitting around moping? She's even wearing colors now. *Colors.* We could all learn a thing or two from Frankie."

While the rest of my family looked stunned, Frankie looked pleased, a tentative smile curving her lips.

I pointed at Missy. "And you—"

Missy threw up her arms and looked at the ceiling. "Can't we all just get along?"

Everyone laughed. Everyone except Jack.

"I liked her better when she wrote that column," Jack said, wiping his mouth with his napkin.

I held up my hands to regain their attention. "There's a difference between maturity and living like a corpse." I gestured to Jack. "No offense."

"None taken," Jack said, pushing away from the table. "Thanks for dinner, Mr. and Mrs. Halladay." He excused himself, getting out while he could.

Who could blame him?

My mother, however, remained seated, moisture shimmering in her eyes.

"I'm sorry, Mom." Shame swirled in the pit of my stomach. Who was I to tell my family how to live their lives? "I was out of line."

But Mom simply shook her head. "I'm not crying because I'm upset."

"You're not?"

She stood, working her way around the table to where I stood. Then she cupped my chin in her hand. "I'm crying because you're right." She held up a finger and headed for the stairs. "Hang on a second."

The rest of us shared puzzled glances as she vanished. Dad dug back into his lasagna. After all, it was amazing. Missy reached for Jack's half-empty iced tea glass and unceremoniously dumped its contents into her milk, creating a seriously unappetizing brown sludge. Nan sat and stared, as if my words had hit her hardest of all.

"Nan?" I leaned for her hand across the table, but Mom returned before I had a chance to say anything more.

"We need a picture," she said, gesturing for us to gather by the dining room wall. She meticulously adjusted the settings on the Minolta, then propped the camera on the table. She studied us as we stood—me with my arms around Nan and Frankie, Dad holding Missy on his hip, Missy holding up her glass of sludge for posterity.

Mom smiled—a luminous, joy-filled smile that creased the skin around her eyes and warmed me to the depths of my soul. A smile just like the one in her old photograph…maybe even better.

She took a deep breath and pressed the timer. "Ten seconds."

Mom dashed to where we stood and slipped her arm around Dad's waist, pressing close to the rest of us—her family. I tightened my hold on Nan and Frankie, wondering when the last time was we'd taken a family picture, if ever.

After the camera snapped off the shot, Mom took another, just to be safe. Then she moved close to whisper in my ear. "You know that picture you gave me?"

I nodded.

"This moment trumps that moment, hands down."

CHAPTER THIRTY-ONE

A short while later, Nan tapped on the door frame of my room. I'd been playing Mom's words over and over again in my mind, looking at page after page of my wedding binder.

I will not sit back and watch you pretend the last month never happened.

I shut the book and pulled the cover insert free of the binder's plastic sleeve.

Abby and Fred.

Nan, much to her credit, made no comment as she stepped inside my bedroom, although I knew she secretly longed to rip the piece of paper to shreds.

"Can you give me a lift?" she asked.

Disbelief washed over me. "Seriously?" I asked. "After all that?"

She sat beside me on the bed and stroked my hair. "Seriously," she answered. "After all that."

I grabbed Dad's fedora from my bureau and tucked my cell phone in the pocket of my jeans. Then I linked arms with my grandmother and steered her down the stairs and toward the back door.

The night had gone chilly and crisp, the scent of spring flowers hanging softly like a tease of things to come.

"I don't have to call you Gus again, do I?" I asked, taking in the jacket she wore—Grandpa's favorite brown corduroy, complete with suede elbow patches.

Nan did her best to look surprised by my question, but I was no dummy. I saw my own fear of change reflected in her eyes.

"Can't a lady wear a jacket when it's chilly outside?" she asked.

"Sure." I opened the passenger door and waited for her to slide inside the cab. "But when she's also dodging phone calls from a certain perfectly charming gentleman, I start thinking she's plain chicken."

Nan's eyes popped wide. She opened her mouth to make her rebuttal just as I slammed the door shut. I held a hand to my ear and mouthed the word *what?*

I took my time making my way around Bessie, pretending to check the car's luminous surface for dirt or scratches. By the time I opened the driver's door and climbed inside, Nan sat with her arms crossed, not saying a word.

She let out a little huff as we pulled away from the curb, and I did my best not to grin.

"It's not polite to call your elders 'chicken,'" she said, turning away from me to stare out the window.

I drove at a snail's pace, taking the turns from Third Avenue to Stone Lane, from Second Avenue to Race as slowly as possible, wanting to squeeze as much time as I could out of our short drive to the library.

"Seems to me," I said, as I drove past the library and pulled Bessie to a stop just outside the Paris Cemetery gates, "you and I aren't so different."

Nan cut her eyes in my direction, arms still firmly crossed, chin tipped upward defiantly. "Go on."

"We're both scared to let go of the past," I said.

She turned to face me, color flushing her cheeks. Either the corduroy was a bit too warm or I'd hit a nerve. "I'd hardly compare my marriage to your grandfather to your engagement to that Fred."

I smiled and reached for her hand, pulling her arm free of her defensive posture. I cradled her slight hand in both of mine, ignoring the pang inside me that registered the fact that she was growing frailer, even though she'd always been larger than life to me.

"I'm not talking only about 'that Fred,'" I said. "I'm talking about my column, my house, my plans. Work with me."

One silver brow lifted toward her hairline. "Jack Maxwell might have a point. I think I liked the whole if-you-can't-say-any-thing-nice phase better than the new blunt phase."

I laughed, a single burst of honest emotion. "You hated that phase, and you know it."

She huffed out another breath. "Perhaps." Her lips quirked into a smile, but she did her best to hide it. "What's with the 'There's a difference between maturity and living like a corpse?' Dr. Phil?"

I shook my head. "Destiny Jones."

Nan chuckled and rolled her eyes. "Oh, brother."

I gave her hand a pat and pushed open my door. "I'm going to walk you to Grandpa's grave; then I'll go get your tea. You think about what I said."

She frowned. "I'm not entirely sure what you did say."

"I have a feeling you'll figure it out."

A few minutes later, I left Nan at Grandpa's grave and made my way down the sidewalk toward the library. Bessie sat parked back by the Paris Cemetery gates, all the simpler to drive Nan home after her visit.

But when I walked through the automatic doors at the library and made the turn for the café, there stood Don Michaels, holding two large to-go cups as he stared in my direction.

Surprise spread across his features, but then his gaze darkened. "Where is she?" he asked. Then his expression tensed. "Is she all right?"

"She will be." I pointed at the cups. "And this?"

He shrugged, looking momentarily like a sixteen-year-old boy about to ask the girl of his dreams to the movies. "If you can't beat 'em, join 'em."

I envisioned Nan and Don sitting together beside Grandpa's grave, sipping hot tea. Oddly enough, I thought Grandpa might enjoy the additional company. I knew he'd enjoy seeing Nan happy again, if only she'd give Don a chance.

I turned sideways and made a sweeping gesture toward the library exit. "Fourth family plot on the right. Can't miss it."

The smile on Don's face was almost as bright as the twinkle in his eyes. He pressed a quick kiss to my cheek and made a beeline for the door.

If anyone could break through Nan's defenses, Don could.

After he left, I headed back outside, turning right instead of left. I cut across the grass toward the Paris Elementary playground and sank down onto the first swing.

I planted my feet in the sand and thought about Max Campbell's offer. Then I took a deep breath and pulled my phone from my pocket.

While the position he'd offered might provide me with a financial boost, I needed more. Lots more.

I needed a career choice that was mine, not another hand-me-down column. I could imagine what Fred would say. He'd tell me to snatch up "Obituaries and Celebrations" and start channeling the voice of the former editor.

But I'd finally reached a point where what Fred said didn't matter.

I didn't want someone else's section. I didn't want someone else's career.

I wanted my career. My risk. My failure. My reward.

All my life, I'd wanted to freelance feature stories and investigative pieces. I hadn't pursued my dream because the uncertainty hadn't fit my plans.

If Max didn't want my ideas for the *Times*, surely some managing editor at another newspaper or magazine would.

There was no better way to encourage Nan to let go of her past than to start letting go of my own.

I called Max, got his voice mail, and left a message wishing him luck in filling the position. Then I extended my legs to push off from the compacted ground beneath the swing.

I sailed backward, bending my legs on the upswing, extending them on the downswing. Before I knew it, I flew through the air.

Backward. Forward. Higher. Faster.

My heart pumped with the exertion and excitement. The wind blasted through my hair and cooled my cheeks, yet I felt myself warm from the inside out.

I tipped back my chin and counted stars, reveling in the simplicity and complexity of their beauty and allure.

Some people lived lives of great moments. Some lived lives of mediocre moments. Some didn't live at all.

During the past month in Paris, I'd learned to live wondrous, breathless, everyday moments.

And those were the most magical moments of all.

CHAPTER THIRTY-TWO

— — —

My room was still dark the next morning when Mom shook my shoulder. "It's Detta."

Her words catapulted me out of my dream and into the reality of her tone and the early-morning hour.

"What's wrong?" I asked, scrambling out from beneath my covers.

"We think it's a stroke," she answered. "Nan's going to stay with Missy. Your dad went with Mick."

I pulled on a pair of jeans and haphazardly shoved my nightgown into the waistband before I pulled my sweatshirt over my head.

I trembled, adrenaline and nerves spiking inside me. "How's Mick?" I asked as we raced down the stairs.

Mom only shook her head, saying nothing as she moved to where Frankie stood, face tucked against the wall, shoulders heaving with her sobs.

"Dad took my car." Mom pointed to the credenza as she pulled open the front door and gathered Frankie into her arms. "He left you Bessie."

He'd also left his fedora, but I reached past it, leaving it where it sat.

I wrapped my fingers around the cab keys and followed Mom and Frankie out into the darkness of early morning, filled with an overwhelming sense of urgency, as if my body already knew what my mind had yet to grasp.

Detta O'Malley regained consciousness long enough to tell Mick she loved him, long enough to tell him he was a good son.

She never lived to see her scrapbook or to see her granddaughter again. The bleeding from her stroke, her doctors explained, was too massive for her brain to survive.

She slipped away just after dawn, with Mick and my family by her side.

In her moment of lucidity, Detta had given Mick a gift. She'd given him a piece of her heart.

I could only hope that would be enough to carry him through the days that followed.

CHAPTER THIRTY-THREE

—— —— ——

We buried Mrs. O'Malley on a cold Monday morning. I'd left Fred a message after she died, telling him I wouldn't be keeping our Sunday meeting.

I needed to be with my family. And Mick.

Mick had demolished the greenhouse out of anger and grief immediately after his mother's funeral. I left him alone to work out his anger through the physical exertion.

Frankie locked herself in her room, crying softly. Not even Don and Riley were able to draw her out of the isolation of her broken heart.

Mom, Missy, and I dug through the pile of discarded and dead plants Mick had piled by the curb, searching for a sign of life.

The peace lily Mick had lovingly rescued from the street beside Maxwell Mortuary had sprouted a single green stem.

Perhaps Detta had been right all along. Maybe her plants had been destined to bloom again, with a little time and love.

Maybe we all were.

I took the pot to Frankie's room, where she sat cradling the delicate plant in her lap as I wrapped her in my arms and told her how much Mrs. O'Malley had loved her.

She and Mom cleared a space in the living room for the lily's large pot, and Frankie busied herself trimming dead leaves and feeding the soil.

In Paris tradition, the entire town gathered to celebrate Detta's life later that same evening.

We crowded inside the Paris Inn Pub and shared songs and stories, toasts and cheers. Although I found comfort in the outpouring of love, I had yet to spot Mick's face in the crowd.

"He's not here," Destiny whispered from the stool beside me. "You can stop twisting your neck around like some desperate giraffe."

"You have a real way with words. You know that?"

"So I hear," she said, forcing a smile.

Jessica had attended the funeral services earlier, but was home now with Max and Bella, so Destiny and I sat together. As resident after resident took the stage to sing or talk, regret built inside me.

How many times had I sat here, on this very stool, too nervous or upset to lift my voice in song?

I focused on determination and I slid off my stool, waving to where Jerry sat handling the microphone.

"Abby Halladay?" he said, his tone quizzical, as if he wondered how close I'd get to the stage this time before I changed my mind.

But this time I wasn't singing for me. I was singing for Detta. I planned to lift my voice in song for the woman who had known the words even when no one would have thought her capable.

I told Jerry my song selection and climbed the steps to the small stage, feeling a bit like the Little Engine That Could.

I think I can. I think I can.

I gripped the microphone in my hand, smiled at the faces of my family, friends, and neighbors, and froze.

The music began, but I sang nothing.

I said nothing.

I did nothing but wonder how many years it had actually been since I'd stood up here and sung.

Suddenly someone took my hand, startling me. Destiny moved beside me, giving me a conspiratorial wink.

"How do you feel about a duet?" She signaled to Jerry to start the song again.

"I thought this wasn't on your bucket list," I whispered.

She gave my fingers a squeeze. "I'm not up here for me."

Jerry restarted the song, and this time, when the first notes sounded, I held tight to Destiny's hand and sang.

My voice started softly, then grew louder and louder, until before long I stood belting out the first song I'd ever heard Detta O'Malley sing.

"Stars shining bright above you…"

Destiny stood beside me, joining me on the choruses, providing backup, all the while never letting go of my hand.

"Dream a little dream of me…"

As my song filled the enclosed space of the Pub, I said a silent good-bye to Detta O'Malley.

And as I returned to my place at the bar and hoisted my beer in a toast for Mick's mother, I said good-bye to sitting on the sidelines.

Once and for all.

CHAPTER THIRTY-FOUR

Early the following afternoon, I found Mick clearing away the pile of rubble that had once been his mother's greenhouse.

His movements slowed as I approached, and in the slump of his shoulders I saw the exhaustion that only grief could place upon a body.

Even though he'd come home to Paris knowing the road would be filled with bumps and free falls and warning cones, Mick thought he'd have more time.

Yet Detta was gone.

I clutched the scrapbook to my chest, sorry that I hadn't taken more pictures, that I hadn't captured more moments.

Mick straightened, pain etched across his face, his eyes full of the grief I'm sure his mother never intended to put there.

"Will you sit with me for a minute?" I asked.

"Where's Fred?" he asked, an emotion I couldn't quite read flashing through his eyes.

"I have no idea," I said honestly.

I hadn't seen Fred since his return from the other Paris. He hadn't returned my message, and I hadn't given him another thought.

I hadn't thought about anything but the man standing before me.

"Please sit with me." I moved to the O'Malleys' back step and sat, giving the concrete beside me a pat.

Mick hesitated before he stripped off his work gloves and strode toward me, his features shifting from exhaustion to defensiveness.

Who could blame him? If I'd suffered the losses he'd suffered in his life, I'd be wearing a full set of armor just to go outside to check the mail.

He sat beside me, and I fought the urge to wrap my arms around him and pull him close. Instead, I released my grip on the scrapbook, set it on his lap, and traced my fingertips across the cover.

I'd slipped a photo of Detta into the front sleeve, choosing one of the shots I'd taken on the morning we ripped out Mom's garden.

In the picture, Detta clutched a fistful of mauve tulips. Her eyes shone with the joy and strength I remembered so vividly from her younger days.

"Do you remember how she used to sneak up to the tree house and leave us food?" Mick's question was barely audible.

I nodded. "She was incredible."

"I miss her."

His words broke my heart, and I fought against the tears that blurred my vision.

"Not just the old her." Mick tapped his finger to the photograph. "This her."

I swallowed down the knot in my throat. "I'm sorry you didn't have more time."

He dropped his chin, looking down at the ground.

"Here." I reached to flip open the first page. "Mom and I put this together for your mother, but we hadn't finished it yet."

Mick refocused on the book and the images of the first time Don and Riley visited.

"These aren't the best ones," I said, turning ahead two pages.

Next were the photographs taken during our picnic. In them, Detta's face appeared relaxed and happy, as if she'd been transported to a time when she hadn't a care in the world.

I turned the page, revealing a photo spread devoted to Detta and Frankie as they sang together one sunny, spring afternoon.

I reached to turn the next page, but Mick placed his hand atop mine.

"Why did you do this?" he asked.

I remained motionless, letting the weight of his touch press against my skin.

"I wanted to save her moments," I said.

"Her moments?"

I nodded. "She had that amazing moment in Dad's cab when she sang, and she knew all of the words. She was so happy."

I turned to study the line of his jaw and the way his eyelashes splayed against his cheeks as he fought to hide his pain.

"But a few minutes later, she'd lost it," I continued. "I could remember how happy she'd been, but she couldn't. I wanted to help her keep her moments, even if they were only in pictures."

Mick shut the book and pushed to his feet, keeping hold of my hand as he pulled me up beside him. My pulse quickened, and I trembled with nerves.

"Take a walk with me," he said.

We cut between yards, crossed Third Avenue on a diagonal, then turned down Stone Lane. We silently walked the two blocks to Bridge Street before he steered me left toward Artisan Alley.

The streets and sidewalks of Paris were empty, and I wondered momentarily if this were another of my dreams in which Mick would vanish as soon as I'd found him.

Neither of us a said a word as we walked, our hands clasped tightly, as if neither of us wanted to let go.

A chill had slipped into the air, and the sun had shifted toward the edge of town and the trees that lined the river.

Partway down Artisan Alley, we stopped in front of the Paris Gallery. Mick tipped his head toward the window, where a display of stained glass dazzled with its brilliance and beauty.

Where before there had been only a handful of pieces, there now hung countless designs and splashes of color, filling the entire window with a beauty that stole both my breath and my words.

And while there were countless floral designs—tulips, daffodils, hydrangeas—it was the stars that left me spellbound.

Varied in size and shape and color, stained-glass stars hung at staggered heights, stunning in their combination of color and pattern.

"Are these yours?" I asked.

Mick nodded. "My mother taught me the process when I was in high school, but after I ran away, I never touched stained glass again."

"Until you came home."

He nodded. "Until I came home."

I pressed my fingers to the window. "They're amazing."

"I needed you to see this." He spoke without turning to face me. We stood, shoulder to shoulder, staring at the beauty of his creativity. "What do you think that means?" he asked.

His voice broke on his last word, and his vulnerability was almost my undoing.

I think I might love you.

The realization slammed my system like a ton of bricks, spiraling through me and weighing me down with that one simple truth.

I love Mick. I always have.

I wanted to scream but instead only stood there, saying, "You always did love show-and-tell."

Mick let out a slight laugh, and I wondered whether he knew me well enough to know what I'd really been thinking.

"Do you think about that night?" he asked.

His question took me by surprise, and yet I knew what he meant. The kiss. The fire. The arrest.

"I tried not to for a long time," I said.

I sneaked a sideways glance, spotting the upturned curve of his lips.

"I hadn't thought about it in years," he said. "And then you pulled up in your parents' drive, and I haven't thought about much else since."

Mick's words floored me, knocking me to my emotional knees.

"Why did you lie for me?" I asked.

"Why did you let me?" he answered.

A beat of silence stretched between us. "I had that coming." I wrapped my arms around my waist to steady myself. "I'm sorry."

But Mick only turned to face me. "Don't be. I wanted to protect you." He cupped my chin and smiled—a tight, cautious smile. "Crazy, huh?"

Not crazy, I thought, realizing that all I'd thought about since Detta died was protecting Mick.

"What will you do now?" I asked.

He grasped my shoulders and I felt transported back to that fateful night at the Bainbridge Estate when I'd kissed him.

In that moment, I'd wanted to stay frozen in time forever, knowing with all the certainty of a seventeen-year-old heart that no one would ever kiss me that way again.

Perhaps that seventeen-year-old had been smarter than I'd given myself credit for.

"What if I said I wanted to build a life here?" Mick asked.

I blinked, wanting to beg him to stay, wanting to tell him I'd fallen in love with him. But instead, I focused on Mick and the one thing I knew he needed to heal his heart.

I reached for his cheek, tracing my fingertips along the lines of tension that stress and grief had left behind. "I think you should go to Seattle and tell Lily her bedtime story in person."

Mick's features tensed and his eyes shimmered with sudden moisture.

"I think you should take Detta's scrapbook and tell Lily about her grandmother," I continued. I lifted up on my toes and kissed his cheek, cursing myself silently as emotion caught in my throat and a tear slid down my cheek. "I think you should go be the dad your father never was. The dad you already are"—I tapped his chest—"right here."

Mick dropped his focus to the scrapbook he still clutched in one hand, yet he said nothing.

For once in my life, I knew I was right. Absolutely, positively right, no matter how much my heart hurt at the thought of Mick walking out of my life again.

"Mick?"

He looked at me, inhaling sharply.

"There may be some things in life you can't fix," I said. "But this one, you can."

"Going to the Chapel" rang out sharply, shattering both the quiet and the moment.

Why on earth hadn't I changed my ringtone or left my phone anywhere but in the front pocket of my jeans?

In Mick's eyes, all signs of open emotion evaporated. His protective shield slid firmly back into place.

I fumbled in my pocket for my phone, silencing the ringer.

The damage, however, had already been done.

Mick straightened, gave me a sharp nod, and turned away. "Thanks for the book," he called out.

I thought about going after him, but instead I stood there, watching him walk away even as the beauty of his stained glass sparkled and shimmered in the window beside me.

I thought about counting the stars, but could only muster the strength to watch Mick until he turned the corner and disappeared from my sight.

I took a step to follow but stopped myself.

I needed to let Mick go. That was the right thing to do.

He needed to walk away. He needed to leave me, Paris, and his memories behind.

He needed to go get Lily and build their life together.

For once in my life, I'd done the right thing.

So while a secret part of me hoped what had just happened might be another of my dreams, the rest of me knew my heart hurt too much for this moment to be anything but real.

CHAPTER THIRTY-FIVE

—— —— ——

By the time I woke the next morning, Mick was gone.

He'd closed up the house during the night, and my dad had driven him to the airport for a six a.m. flight to Seattle.

I'd watched them leave, staring out the window as Bessie's taillights disappeared at the end of Third Avenue.

I supposed it was better this way. I'd survived Mick's sudden departure once. I could survive it again.

Dad had made blueberry muffins to soften the blow, but all I could do was sit on our back step and stare at the empty space in the O'Malleys' backyard where the greenhouse had stood just a few days earlier.

The screen door creaked behind me, and Nan emerged from the house, wearing an oversize cardigan that looked suspiciously like one I'd seen Don wear on his last visit.

She sat beside me and wrapped her arm around my waist, pulling me close like she used to do when I was no more than Missy's age.

"You okay?" she asked.

I nodded slowly. "I will be."

"For what it's worth, Macaroon, I think you did the right thing."

I'd confided to my parents and Nan the night before, feeling a bit like a teenager spilling her guts. It had felt good to share my feelings with the people I loved most, and they'd listened without judgment.

I wanted to answer Nan's question, but I was afraid that if I tried to talk, I'd start crying. And once I started crying, I feared I'd never be able to stop.

"I think it's a rare gift to love someone so much you encourage them to do what they need to do, even though you know it's going to break your heart," Nan said.

Much as I tried to hold them back, my tears came. Understated in their arrival, they slid down my face and dripped off my chin just the same.

Nan handed me a tissue.

I blew my nose, the noise not in any way graceful or ladylike.

Nan patted my shoulder before she pushed to her feet. "Special Clipper meeting at your house today," she said. "Better get a move on."

I looked up at her and frowned, completely confused by what she'd said. "At my house? Why?"

She smiled a gentle smile that somehow soothed the rough edges of my soul. "Guess you'll have to show up to find out."

A few minutes later, Nan and I piled into Bessie and headed for Second Avenue.

I carefully maneuvered Bessie down the street, making a wide turn into my driveway. My blue Beetle sat all but forgotten next to Destiny's van.

Destiny stood at the top of the drive, hands on hips, sporting the biggest smile I'd ever seen.

I parked the car, and Nan climbed out faster than I'd seen her move in years. I followed, my own steps a bit more cautious.

Suspicion tapped at the base of my brain. "What's going on?" I asked.

Destiny shrugged, holding out her hand. "Guess you'll have to come inside to find out."

I followed her around back to the kitchen door, where coffee and boxes of doughnuts sat along the counter. The floor gleamed, refinished to a gorgeous shine.

Numerous voices sounded from the living room, falling silent as someone yelled out, "She's here."

I laughed, disbelief washing over me. "You know, it's not my birthday."

"It might as well be," Destiny said, moving behind me and giving me a solid push through the door.

There before me stood Mom, Dad, Missy, Frankie, Mona Capshaw, Manny, Ted Miller, and most every other Clipper, if I weren't mistaken.

Jessica crossed the room to give my arm a squeeze, holding a fat paintbrush out to her side.

"Who's running the town?" I joked, but the truth was, I'd never been so touched by the kindness of others in my life.

Destiny and I had gone over colors during the weekend. I'd expected to spend much of this week painting, yet here my home stood—restored, polished, and painted to perfection.

"When did you do this?" I asked.

"Many hands make light work," Nan answered.

"Plus"—Mona stepped out from the pack—"we old folks don't sleep much."

A warm gold covered the living room walls, and the radiators had not only been reinstalled, they'd been painted a beautiful antique white.

The baseboards and crown molding had also been painted antique white, as had the wood trim that framed my home's enormous windows.

I fought the urge to pinch myself, but I also found it nearly impossible to speak.

"How can I ever repay you?" I asked, looking first at Destiny and Rock, then at the Clippers and my family.

"Argh," Mona Capshaw said. "Consider this a perk of living in Paris."

Frank Turner stepped forward and shook my hand. "Looks like you're ready to move in. Destiny did an amazing job."

Move in.

A month ago that had been my only thought. Now, I couldn't stop thinking about how long it might take to drive to Seattle.

Ted Miller shook my hand, smiling. "I still say you should think about pharmacy tech if you want to pay your half of the mortgage."

"Thanks, Ted," I murmured, laughing as the rest of the Clippers lined up to shake my hand, pat my back, or envelop me in a hug.

"Does anybody have a—"

But there was no need to finish my question. Mom worked the room, snapping pictures on the old Minolta as if she'd been a photographer all her life.

Dad stepped forward and kissed my cheek. "It's beautiful, honey."

"Thanks, Dad."

"Do you think you'll keep it?" he asked.

I blew out a sigh. "I can't afford this house on my own."

Hell, Fred didn't even know about the changes I'd made. Then I realized, Destiny and I might have found most of the materials at the salvage yard, but the paint and other supplies hadn't been free.

I pulled Destiny aside and dropped my voice low as everyone else headed to the kitchen for refreshments. "I need to pay you for this."

"No, you don't." She shook her head, shoving a wayward strand of mahogany hair up under her painter's cap. "Coupons, baby. It's all about the coupons."

"You mean to tell me…"

Then I remembered the bigger-than-usual Clipper meetings recently.

"We combined forces to find you the materials you needed for next to nothing," Destiny continued. "Maybe now you'll reconsider that booty pack."

I laughed, wanting to stand inside this room, surrounded by Clippers, savoring this moment forever.

Missy tugged at my sleeve. "There's something for you in the kitchen."

"More? I was just in there."

I followed my little sister back into the kitchen.

Frankie stood in front of the kitchen window, her eyes bright, palpable joy edging out the lines of grief on her young face.

I was about to tell her how happy I was to see her smile when she stepped to one side, providing me with a clear view of the window's glass panes.

There hung a stained-glass star, its facets and angles an intricate design of blue, amber, lavender, pale green, and yellow. Each cut was perfect, with the exception of the star's focal point—a pale-green glass triangle, its beauty flawed by a single crack.

"We heard he took off again," Frank Turner said.

I held up my hands before anyone could say another word. "He has something he needs to do."

"I'm amazed he had the nerve to show his face again in the first place after he burned down the Paris Oak."

I had no idea who'd made the comment, but I had to make it stop.

I had always loved the point in a movie where the heroine had to decide whether or not to fight for what she believed. The time had come for me to fight for Mick.

The time had come for me to tell the truth.

I hoisted my hands higher into the air, waiting for the chatter to die down.

I drew in a deep breath, I concentrated on steadying the beat of my heart, and then I chose my words carefully, speaking them slowly and clearly.

"I burned down the tree."

The room went silent.

"Mick lied to protect me."

Mona clucked her tongue. "It's a little late to defend him now."

I pushed past the shame that washed through me. "You're right. I should have defended him thirteen years ago. And if it makes you feel better, you can go engrave my name in that big rock where the tree once stood."

Destiny stared. Jessica stared. My mother had gone pale. The Clippers stood uncharacteristically silent.

Ted Miller opened his mouth, and I gave him the palm-in-the-air-please-don't-utter-a-single-syllable sign he was probably getting used to.

Frank shrugged. "This is a first."

I frowned. "For what?"

Frank laughed. "A secret in Paris. Who'd have thought it possible?"

Nan, who had never said a negative thing to me in my life, stepped forward and hooked her fingers beneath my chin. "Macaroon, you're an idiot."

Mona laughed. Jessica laughed. My mother laughed, and before long, the entire group laughed, their tone shifting from one of nervous disbelief to one of love and forgiveness.

I laughed along with them, my joy and relief building from the pit of my belly, lightening my burden as it moved upward and outward after being held inside me for so many years.

"Yes," I said. "Yes, I am."

CHAPTER THIRTY-SIX

A few moments later, Destiny made her way to my side, hooked my elbow, and dragged me toward the home's front window.

Fred Newton walked up the sidewalk toward the yellow Victorian, and I stood frozen in place, as if I were watching a movie reel unwind before my eyes.

My stomach flipped and my heart fell to my toes.

I'd been laughing and celebrating as if this house were mine, when the truth was, it was half Fred's. This house was part of the life we'd planned before everything had changed.

As he drew near, Fred looked nothing like the man I remembered. He looked smaller, a less significant part of my world somehow.

While I knew I should be worried about his reaction to the house and how much renovation I'd approved without his input, his wasn't the name echoing through my brain. His wasn't the face playing across my mind. His welfare wasn't the worry haunting my every waking moment.

I'd let Mick go because he needed to go, but as I watched Fred approach, I wondered if I really needed to stay.

I headed outside and met Fred partway across the home's front yard.

We stood awkwardly facing each other, without as much as a handshake.

"Fred," I said.

"I got your messages," he said.

No hug. No kiss. No apology.

"Sorry I had to cancel on Sunday," I said.

He smiled, the move stiff. "No problem. I figured today might be a good day to drive down to see you."

I thought about saying countless things. I thought about yelling at him for leaving me, for walking out two months before our wedding. I thought about saying a lot of things, but instead, I said nothing.

"I had to go, Abby," he said.

"Did you?" I asked.

Then I realized, maybe he did need to go. Maybe he'd needed to seize the exceptional moments of his life by heading to France, but he could have been a bit more thoughtful in his departure.

Unlike Mick, who had left once to protect me and get away from his father, and once to go after his daughter, Fred had left for purely selfish reasons.

"Why didn't you tell me you were unhappy?" I asked.

He shrugged. "I think I was afraid."

"Of me?"

He nodded. "Of messing up your plans."

I blew out a breath, eerily calm. "You could have returned at least one of my messages."

Fred shook his head. "I took a vow of silence."

I blinked.

"What's with the hat?" He pointed to Dad's fedora.

"Don't change the subject."

"Sorry."

A vow of silence.

"So what did you do?" I asked. "Become a monk?"

Fred shook his head again; then he placed his palms in the air, building an invisible wall to his front, his left, his right.

My gut tightened. Surely, he didn't—

"I became a mime." He beamed as he spoke the words, as if he'd found his true calling.

"Are you fucking kidding me?"

He staggered backward and did an exaggerated finger waggle to chastise me.

"Shut up, Fred."

He opened his mouth as if shocked, flattening his palms to his cheeks.

I closed the small space between us and grabbed his hands, pulling them down to his sides. His eyes popped wider, much as I hadn't thought that possible.

"Do you love me, Fred?"

He pursed his lips and tipped his head to one side.

I resisted the urge to smack him. Having never been a violent person, I didn't think this was a good time to start. Plus, we'd drawn a crowd.

Mom, Dad, Nan, and Frankie stood on the front lawn, surrounded by Clippers. Destiny and Jessica stood a few steps closer to me, poised as if ready to do battle.

Missy, who had obviously overheard, walked beside us, pantomiming as if she were pulling herself down the sidewalk along an invisible rope.

"Do you love me?" I repeated, this time much more softly.

Fred blinked, and in that millisecond I saw the truth.

"I didn't think so." My voice grew thick with emotion, even though I knew I didn't love him either.

For a split second, I thought about the time I'd lost while I'd been with Fred, but then I realized something. Without him, we might never have bought the little Victorian, and I might never have returned to Paris.

Sure, we had the issue of our shared house and mortgage to deal with, but as I glanced over my shoulder and took a mental picture of my family, friends, and Clippers, I realized that without the plans Fred and I had made, I might never have found this moment.

"Why did you come see me?" I asked.

"To say good-bye."

We stared at each other for what seemed like forever, and then we both smiled.

"Good-bye, Fred." I pushed to my tiptoes and kissed his cheek.

"Good-bye, Abby."

I released my grip on his hands and ran, scooping Missy into my arms as I crossed the yard, back toward Bessie.

"Who wants to drive me to the airport?"

CHAPTER THIRTY-SEVEN

—— —— ——

I stood at the door between my arrival gate and baggage claim and read the posted sign.

No Reentry.

I flexed my fingers, trying to ease the ache six hours of white-knuckling armrests had left behind. Then I stepped forward.

No Reentry.

No worries. I had no intention of turning back.

Little more than a month ago, I thought I'd do whatever it took to save the life I'd planned, yet here I stood, ready to risk my heart and my future on a life I'd never imagined.

Life was a journey of letting go.

Life was about learning to adjust, learning to accept the disappointments, the unexpected developments, and the out-of-this-world-wonderful surprises.

Life was about appreciating life—with all its flaws and quirks and challenges. Life was about embracing the everyday moments and owning whatever happened next.

I pulled Dad's hat out of the duffel bag I'd thrown together before my entire family had driven me to the airport. I'd tried to give the fedora back to my father, but he'd insisted I take it for good luck.

In the excitement of catching the next plane to Seattle, I hadn't had time to do much more than pack and run. I supposed if I'd had more time to think, I might never have boarded the plane. But once the door was shut and the seat belt sign was illuminated, I was committed…and trapped.

It hadn't been pretty, but I'd distracted myself by thinking about how much I'd miss my family.

Moving back home had given me a chance to see them in an entirely new light, and I wouldn't trade a single, wonderful moment.

I'd given my house keys to Destiny, suggesting she and Rock use the Victorian as a showroom for the time being.

If I stayed in Seattle, and Fred and I sold the property, maybe Don would decide to buy the little yellow house on Second Avenue. I had it on good authority that it had been recently renovated.

Mom had asked if she could turn my old bedroom into a studio, now that I was moving out again.

About time.

So there I stood, at the perimeter of baggage claim, silently praying Mick wanted to see me as much as I wanted to see him.

Was I crazy? Maybe.

I pulled the fedora down over my hair and powered on my phone. I waited, hoping Mick had gotten the text I'd sent before I left Newark, hoping he cared.

He'd left my dad his cell phone number in case anything came up regarding his mother's house. Dad, having always been a fan of Mick's, had handed me the digits before he kissed me good-bye.

The phone illuminated in my hand, displaying the family portrait Mom had taken. Wallpaper only. No waiting messages.

My heart sank, but I knew I'd done the right thing by facing my fear and hopping on a plane.

I was through letting life pass me by, even if I got my heart broken in the process.

Then my phone vibrated in my hand.

New text message. Mick O'Malley.

I held my breath as I ran my fingertip across the screen to reveal the words beneath.

Nice hat, Halladay.

My face crumpled, and I didn't care how hard I cried, or what anyone thought.

A man clipped me with a rolling bag as he rushed past, and I fought to keep my balance as I looked up.

I searched for Mick, scanning the faces in the crowd, my heart slamming against my ribs, my pulse roaring in my ears.

Maybe one day Mick and I would return to Paris. Maybe we'd spend the rest of our lives together in Seattle. Maybe we wouldn't end up together at all.

But when I saw him, my every thought of making plans faded away.

Mick.

He handed his phone to an apparent stranger and pointed in my direction. Then he closed the space between us, pulled me into his arms, and kissed me.

The rest of the world went silent, and I wondered if it would be wrong to stay like this forever, kissing like two fools in the middle of the Sea-Tac International baggage claim.

Somewhere in the periphery of my awareness, his phone's flash illuminated. Mick laughed, and his soft breath warmed my cheek.

"What took you so long?" he whispered.

I had no way of knowing what our future might bring, but there was one thing of which I was absolutely certain.

That moment—*our moment*—was absolutely perfect.

NOTE TO READERS

— — —

Dear Reader,

Thank you for picking up a copy of *Changing Lanes*. I appreciate you!

Are you a member of a book club or readers group? If so, please let me know if you'd like to receive bookmarks, signed bookplates, or other goodies. Drop me a line at kathleen@ kathleenlong.com with the words BOOK CLUB in the subject line.

Also, I love chatting with readers groups! If you'd like me to visit via phone or Skype, let me know when you'll be discussing *Changing Lanes*—or any of my other titles—and I'll do my best to make the dates work. If your group is local to me, I'd love to visit you in person.

When you e-mail me, please let me know a little about your group. When did you start meeting? Where do you meet? How many members are in your club? And please send me a photo. I'd love to include your smiling faces on my wall of readers!

Thanks once more for your wonderful support of *Changing Lanes*. I look forward to talking with you soon!

With warmest wishes,
Kathleen

Be sure to catch *Chasing Rainbows*,
a *USA Today* bestseller!

In life, you either choose to sing a rainbow, or you don't.
For Bernie, the singing is about to begin.

Available now on Amazon.com.

ACKNOWLEDGMENTS

For my editor, Lindsay Guzzardo, thank you for your enthusiasm, patience, and encouragement as I developed the fictional world of Paris, New Jersey, for *Changing Lanes*. For my developmental editor, Tiffany Yates Martin, whose skill, insight, and wisdom helped me deepen Abby's story while allowing my voice and intent to remain intact, I appreciate you more than you'll ever know.

For the readers, bloggers, reviewers, and friends who embraced *Chasing Rainbows* and helped make this author's dreams come true, thank you! Your e-mails, letters, and friendships mean the world to me. I hope *Changing Lanes* and the story of Abby Halladay's lessons in letting go will strike an emotional chord and resonate with you long after you've turned the last page.

Last—but certainly not least—for Dan and Annie, I love you! It takes a special, supportive, and slightly crazy crew to understand and encourage my late-night hours, writing quirks, and endless scribbling of notes. For all of this and so much more, thank you from the bottom of my heart. I truly could not do any of this without you.

ABOUT THE AUTHOR

Photo © Lee Isbell, Studio 16, 2005

Kathleen Long is the RITA®-nominated author of more than a dozen novels of contemporary romance, romantic suspense, and women's fiction. In addition to a RIO Award and two Gayle Wilson Awards of Excellence, her writing accolades include National Readers Choice, Holt Medallion, Booksellers Best, and Book Buyers Best award nominations, as well as appearances on the *USA Today* and *Wall Street Journal* bestseller lists. When she isn't writing, she dabbles in jewelry design and child- and puppy-wrangling. A Delaware native, she divides her time between Philadelphia and the Jersey Shore.